VOLU

A Macabre Vision

Something in a corner caught his eye. A big box. He turned the beam on it. It was a coffin. He walked to it. He did not remember its being there when he visited this place before. The coffin was not old. It was new.

He opened the lid. Inside was the usual satin lining, nothing else. He touched the lining. Thought these cellars were cool and damp, the lining was warm.

Someone, something, had been in there and very recently. It was dark outside when the vampires roamed. He meditated for a moment. Then Devil growled. . .

Hermes Press

Published by Hermes Press, an imprint of Herman and Geer Communications, Inc.
Daniel Herman, Publisher
Troy Musguire, Production Manager
Eileen Sabrina Herman, Managing Editor
Alissa Fisher, Graphic Design
Kandice Hartner, Senior Editor
Benjamin Beers, Archivist

2100 Wilmington Road
Neshannock, Pennsylvania 16105
(724) 652-0511
www.HermesPress.com; info@hermespress.com

Cover image: Painting of The Phantom by George Wilson
Book design by Eileen Sabrina Herman
First printing, 2019

LCCN Applied For: 10 9 8 7 6 5 4 3 2 1 0
ISBN 978-1-61345-179-3
OCR and text editing by H + G Media and Eileen Sabrina Herman
Proof reading by Eileen Sabrina Herman and Kandice Hartner

From Dan, Louise, Sabrina, Ruckus, and Noodle for D'zur and Mellow

Acknowledgements: This book would not be possible without the help, cooperation, patience, and kindness of many people. First and foremost in making this endeavor a reality are Ita Golzman and Frank Caruso at King Features. Thanks also to Pete Klaus and the late Ed Rhoades of "The Friends of the Phantom." Pete and Ed have provided us with resource material, contacts, information, and helpful insights into the strip and continue to be there when we have questions about the world of The Ghost Who Walks.

Editor's Note: There were several misspellings in the original text; those have been corrected with this reprint. However, the alternate spelling for the Singh pirates as Singg was kept to preserve the original format.

Printed in Canada

The Story of THE PHANTOM and The Vampire and the Witch

Lee Falk

CONTENTS

PROLOGUE

How It All Began

Over four hundred years ago, a large British merchant ship was attacked by Singg pirates off the remote shores of Bangalla. The captain of the trading vessel was a famous seafarer who, in his youth, had served as cabin boy to Christopher Columbus on his first voyage to discover the New World. With the captain was his son, Kit, a strong young man who idolized his father and hoped to follow him as a seafarer. But the pirate attack was disastrous. In a furious battle, the entire crew of the merchant ship was killed and the ship sank in flames. The sole survivor was young Kit who, as he fell off the burning ship, saw his father killed by a pirate. Kit was washed ashore, half-dead. Friendly pygmies found him and nursed him to health.

One day, walking on the beach, he found a dead pirate dressed in his fathers clothes. He realized this was the pirate who had killed his father. Grief-stricken, he waited until vultures had stripped the body clean. Then on the skull of his father's murderer, he swore an oath by firelight as the pygmies watched. "I swear to devote my life to the destruction of piracy, greed, cruelty, and injustice – and my sons and their sons shall follow me."

This was the Oath of the Skull that Kit and his descendants would live by. In time, the pygmies led him to their home in the Deep Woods in the center of the jungle, where he found a large cave with many rocky chambers. The mouth of the cave, a natural formation formed by the water and wind of centuries, was curiously like a skull. This became his home, the Skull Cave. He soon adopted a mask and a strange costume. He found that the mystery and fear this inspired helped him in his endless battle against world-wide piracy. For he and his sons who followed became known as the nemesis of pirates everywhere, a mysterious man whose face no one ever saw, whose name no one knew, who worked alone.

As the years passed, he fought injustice wherever he found it. The first Phantom and the sons who followed found their wives in many places. One married a reigning queen, one a princess, one a beautiful red-haired barmaid. But whether queen or commoner, all followed their men back to the Deep Woods to live the strange but happy life of the wife of the Phantom. And of all the world, only she, wife of the Phantom and their children, could see his face.

Generation after generation was conceived and born, grew to manhood, and assumed the tasks of the father before him. Each wore the mask and costume. Folk of the jungle and the city and sea began to whisper that there was a man who could not die, a Phantom, a Ghost Who Walks. For they thought the Phantom was always the same man. A boy who saw the Phantom would see him again fifty years after; and he seemed the same. And he would tell his son and his grandson; and then his son and grandson would see the Phantom fifty years after that. And he would seem the same. So the legend grew. The Man Who Cannot Die. The Ghost Who Walks. The Phantom.

The Phantom did not discourage this belief in his immortality. Always working alone against tremendous – sometimes almost impossible – odds, he found that the awe and fear the legend inspired was a great help in his endless battle against evil. Only his friends, the pygmies, knew the truth. To compensate for their tiny stature, the pygmies, mixed deadly poisons for use on their weapons in hunting or defending themselves. It was rare that they were forced to defend themselves. Their deadly poisons were known through the jungle, and they and their home, the Deep Woods, were dreaded and avoided. Another reason to stay away from the Deep Woods – it soon became known that this was a home of the Phantom, and none wished to trespass.

Through the ages, the Phantoms created several more homes, or hideouts, in various parts of the world. Near the Deep Woods was the Isle of Eden, where the Phantom taught all animals to live in peace. In the southwest desert of the New World, the Phantoms created an eyrie on a high, steep mesa that was thought by the Indians to be haunted by evil spirits and became known as "Walker's Table" – for the Ghost Who Walks. In Europe, deep in the crumbling cellars of ancient castle ruins, the Phantom had another hideout from which to strike against evildoers.

But the Skull Cave in the quiet of the Deep Woods remained the true home of the Phantom. Here, in a rocky chamber, he kept his chronicles, written records of all his adventures. Phantom after Phantom faithfully recorded their experiences in the large folio volumes. Another chamber contained the costumes of all the generations of Phantoms. Other chambers contained the vast treasures of the Phantom acquired over the centuries, used only in the endless battle against evil.

Thus twenty generations of Phantoms lived, fought, and died – usually violently – as they fulfilled their oath. Jungle folk, sea folk and city folk believed him the same man, the Man Who Cannot Die. Only the pygmies knew that always, a day would come when their great friend would die. Then, alone, a strong young son would carry his father to the burial crypt of his ancestors where all Phantoms rested. As the pygmies waited outside, the young man would emerge from the cave, wearing the mask, the costume, and the skull ring of the Phantom; his carefree, happy days as the Phantom's son were over. And the pygmies would chant their age-old chant, "The Phantom is dead. Long live the Phantom."

The story of the Vampire and the Witch is an adventure of the Phantom of our time—the twenty-first generation of his line. He has inherited the traditions and responsibilities created by four centuries of Phantom ancestors. One ancestor created the Jungle Patrol. Thus, today, our Phantom is the mysterious and unknown commander of this elite corps. In the jungle, he is known and loved as The Keeper of the Peace. On his right hand is the Skull Ring that leaves his mark— the Sign of the Skull—known and feared by evildoers everywhere. On his left hand—closer to the heart—is his "good mark" ring. Once given, the mark grants the lucky bearer protection by the Phantom, and it is equally known and respected. And to good people and criminals alike in the jungle, on the seven seas, and in the cities of the world he is the Phantom, the Ghost Who Walks, the Man Who Cannot Die.

Lee Falk
New York 1974

CHAPTER 1

The Mawitaan newscaster chuckled as he read the next item to his radio listeners. "In closing, here is our silliest story of the day. No, let's give it the full honor it deserves—the silliest story of the year. It comes from Koqania. You don't know where Koqania is? Neither do I. Someplace in Europe, I think. Look it up in your atlas, as I will. Anyhow, little Koqania—I'm guessing it's little— tells us it is being terrorized by a plague of vampires. Not bats, human vampires. And as if that isn't enough for one day, they go on to say the human vampires are led [the newscaster choked with laughter here], excuse me, are led by a witch. If you kiddies who are listening don't know what a vampire is, well, we don't have any in Bangalla, I hope. Ask your daddy to tell you. Ask him about a witch, too. And those Europeans call us superstitious! Heh, heh. Until tomorrow evening at the same time, this is Segundo Togando saying good night and sweet dreams."

All over black Bangalla, children were readied for bed, and parents explained vampires and witches. Some looked in their atlases for Koqania. They found the tiny nation in an obscure corner of southern Europe, tucked between mountains.

In the depths of the jungle, in the mysterious Deep Woods, a radio clicked off inside the Skull Cave. In one of its chambers, a powerful radio transmitter was set in the rocky wall. Rex, a blond white boy, and Tomm, his black companion, both ten and both clad only in loincloths, sat on the stone floor with Devil, the big gray wolf.

"Uncle Walker, what are vampires and witches?" asked Rex. Rex, a foundling, was growing up in the Deep Woods as the Phantom's ward. This name, "Uncle Walker," which he used for his foster parent, was derived from another name of the Phantom—the Ghost Who Walks.

Standing by the radio panel, the Phantom considered for a moment. Hooded and masked, clad in the skintight costume with two guns hanging from a broad belt that bore his insignia, the Sign of the Skull, he was a powerful, awesome figure to outside eyes. But to these boys and to the little people of the Deep Woods, two of whom stood listening in the shadows of the cave, he was their loving friend and protector.

"Like the man said," he answered, glancing at the radio panel, "they are silly notions and do not really exist."

"But what are they?" persisted Rex.

As the Phantom looked at the eager young faces, he hesitated. It was their bedtime and he didn't want to inspire nightmares. But he'd never refused questions about anything before.

"What is a vampire?" asked a quavering voice from the shadows. "I'd heard tell of witches, more than one, but never of vampires." This was old Mozz, the Bandar teller of tales. Like most primitive people who cannot write, the pygmies depended on their tellers to preserve the oral history of the tribe. Such tellers as Old Mozz knew hundreds, perhaps thousands, of legends, myths, and histories of their people stretching back into antiquity.

"Is vampire a mystery that must remain hidden for the good of the people or can it be told?" asked another voice in the click-clack language of the pygmies. This was Guran, the pygmy chief, the Phantom's oldest friend.

The Phantom laughed. "It is no secret and no mystery, only a foolish notion. I didn't want to give the boys bad dreams, but perhaps it won't as long as they understand that vampires are not real. Vampires are people, men or women, who are said to live on human blood."

"Like spiders or mosquitoes?" said Rex excitedly.

"In a way, but not exactly. The human vampire is said to sleep by day in a hidden coffin at which time he is like a dead person. But at night he wakes up to roam the land searching for victims. It is said that when he finds one and takes his blood, the victim then becomes a vampire as well."

"Perhaps he excretes some manner of poison like the cobra," said Mozz wisely.

"Perhaps," answered the Phantom. "It is said, further, that the vampire will never die, and cannot be killed with bullets or knives, but in only one way. He must be found when asleep in the coffin. Then a wooden stake must be driven into his heart. When this is done, he will fade into dust."

"He lives forever, like the Phantom? Is that so hard to believe?" said Mozz with a dry, rasping chuckle. Guran also laughed. Of all the jungle folk, only the pygmies knew that the Ghost Who Walks was not immortal, and lived and died like an ordinary man.

"That's not so scary," said Rex. "What do they look like? Do they have wings like bats?"

"Like ordinary people, I believe."

"What about witches," said Tomm, who had been listening wide-eyed all the while.

"Old women, who are supposed to perform black magic and put spells on people and the like. They don't exist either," said the Phantom.

"Ah, but is that true?" said Old Mozz who would never contradict the Phantom directly. "The Gooley-Gooley Witch for one, and indeed the Hanta Witch known to your forebears."

"Enough of this talk," said the Phantom. "Off to bed with you."

But the boys, filled with new questions, didn't move.

"The Gooley-Gooley witch?" said Rex excitedly. "Who was she?"

"I said, enough for tonight," said the Phantom, and his tone became sharp, unusual for him with the boys. It was obviously a subject he didn't want to discuss.

"But Uncle Walker," said Rex.

The Phantom bent down and picked up Rex and Tomm from the floor, one with each hand.

"Good night," he said gently but firmly, and they knew the time for argument was over. He kissed each boy, then put them back on the floor. They scampered out of the cave, chattering excitedly to each other.

"That place, Koqania, has special meaning for you?" said Old Mozz whose amazing memory was as enormous and infallible as a computer.

"Yes. Frankly, the broadcast gave me quite a start. In an old ruin of a castle there, we have a place, a hideout," he said. When he used the pronoun "we" he meant the entire line of the Phantoms, all the generations of which he was the twenty-first. He walked along the rocky cave corridor with the bent old Mozz, who moved slowly with the help of a gnarled polished cane. Old Mozz's cloud of white hair and long white beard glistened in the torchlight. Chief Guran, grown stocky and heavy over the years, walked slowly behind them.

"And do you know why you have a place in those ruins of Koqania?" said Old Mozz.

"It seems to me I once knew, but I've forgotten. I was only there once, many years ago."

They were passing a rocky chamber that contained long shelves of large leather-bound folio volumes, the Phantom Chronicles. On these vellum pages, each Phantom from the very beginning had recorded his adventures and the important events of his life—marriage, births, death.

"Look in there. You will find it written," said Old Mozz, gesturing.

"What will I find, you who have heard all and forgotten nothing?" said the Phantom. The old man bowed his head slightly to acknowledge the compliment.

"It is best that you read it for yourself," said Old Mozz with a sly smile. "You will learn something of astonishment." And the old man left the cave. Chief Guran paused at the cave mouth.

"Mozz is a devilish fellow. He could have told, but he wished to leave you puzzled."

"And so he has," said the Phantom.

"If it is anything of astonishment that I can know, will you tell me?" said Guran, as curious as a child.

The Phantom smiled at his boyhood friend.

"I promise," he said. And he turned back toward the chamber containing the Phantom Chronicles. Hidden in there was something of astonishment. What could it be?

CHAPTER 2

Searching for this secret of Koqania, one tale among thousands in these histories of four centuries, was a long task even for the Phantom, who had grown up with these chronicles. From the time his father had first brought him into this chamber and introduced him to the amazing past of his ancestors, he'd spent countless hours with the big books. So he stood now before the podium, reading by torchlight, going through volume after volume, searching for the elusive word, Koqania. And lying at his feet, watching as always with his pale-blue eyes, was Devil, the gray mountain wolf.

Other matters interrupted his reading, and he was to go through a score of volumes before he found what he was looking for. In the meantime, he heard another newscast about Koqania.

"Here we go again. Another report of that plague of vampires led by a witch in Koqania. It is said that fearful peasant farmers are leaving their crops unharvested. Many are fleeing the district Local authorities scoff at the reports as nonsense.

"Amen to that," said the newscaster.

In a chronicle dated April 1675, almost three centuries old, he found the first reference to Koqania, written by his ancestor, the eighth Phantom. (This mighty man was the son of the seventh

Phantom, who had met, bested, and befriended the great black Emperor Joonkoor, and was the grandson of the sixth Phantom and Natala, Queen of France.) Carefully written in a large firm script on the imperishable vellum was the following.

"At the request of my good friend and chess opponent, the Ottoman Sultan Abu Mahoud, I journeyed to Europe to the tiny barony called Koqania. Here, where the rich caravans of my friend and others were forced to travel to reach the marts of the western world, they were seized by beings described as blood-drinking demons and forced to pay tribute to the owner of the castle at the pass, a beauteous witch."

The Phantom paused and almost shivered. A witch at Koqania three hundred years ago? He read on.

"As I neared the mountainous country, I heard tales of the Hanta witch, for that is how they called her. Some said her beauty was so intense that it melted men's bones. Others whispered of the vast tribute she demanded of her captives. If they refused or could not meet her demands, they paid with their lives at the hands of her blood-drinking demons. The more I heard of this matter, the more curious I was to see this beauteous witch of Hanta."

Hanta witch? Hadn't Old Mozz mentioned that name? "The Hanta witch, known to your forebears." Did the amazing old man know everything about the four-hundred-year-old line of the Phantoms? He read on in this chronicle of 1675, written by the Eighth.

"When I reached this remote place called Koqania, I found a wild land of high peaks and swift torrents. Large brown bears and gray wolves roamed the thick woods. I met and was forced to dispatch several. In power and ferocity, they seemed the equal of the great cats of our jungle. The barony was sparsely populated. Hamlets were few. The people were suspicious and hostile, not only to strangers I learned, but to each other as well. A pall of fear seemed to hang over the land. When I tried to question them about the witch at the pass, they slammed their doors shut or set their fierce dogs upon me. But I wasted little time with these rude folk, for I was anxious to see the beauteous witch. At length, I reached her castle. It was a huge ancient edifice, set astride a peak like a great bird of prey. Beneath was the pass through which the caravans must travel to reach the marts. As luck would have it, a battle was in progress when I arrived.

"A caravan from the Levant—a long line of horses, donkeys, and camels with their riders and guards—was at that moment being attacked by a swarm of creatures from the surrounding slopes. They evidently came from the castle. I say 'creatures.' They were all clad in fiery red robes and had the appearance of men with the normal complement of arms and legs. But their heads, under iron helmets, were hideous, resembling the gargoyles on the great cathedrals of Europe. If these were the demons, they were well named, for they fought with an unbelievable fury.

"I watched for several minutes. With their sharp scimitars, they slashed at whatever was closest—men, horses, donkeys, or camels. The caravan guards tried to stem this onslaught, but they were appalled by the fury of these gargoyles, and perhaps by their appearance as well, and began to panic. At that moment, I charged in, a pistol in one hand, my great sword in the other. Surprised, they gave way and started back up the slope, but not before I had dispatched several. I did not stop to talk with the caravan people, but pursued the gargoyles toward the castle; for that was why I had come. The creatures tried to make a stand at several level places on the hill, but I moved through them. If these were the 'blood-drinking demons,' they had no chance to indulge their horrid appetites this time. The only blood-drinking done was by my great sword."

"Wow," said the Phantom aloud as he visualized this daring action by his ancestor. He took a drink of spring water, petted Devil, then returned to the podium to continue the tale.

"I should add for this record," continued the chronicle, "that though these creatures were demonic, demons they were not. During that battle up the slope, several of their gargoyle 'heads' fell off. They were tough masks of some sort that served to protect their heads as well as terrify opponents. The heads beneath belonged to ordinary ruffians, unshaven and unwashed.

"I broke through the outer circle of these fellows and reached the moat. The drawbridge was up. I swam across the moat, noting that it was swarming with various small and loathsome things, some with tentacles, that suited the moat of a witch. I dispatched several bolder creatures with my dagger and reached the wall. As I started to climb, the water below me hissed. Something was being poured down from above. I dodged aside just in time as gray steaming matter fell within inches of me. It was boiling lead. Had it touched me, my flesh would have been reduced to cinders, and I would have joined the creatures in the moat. Fortunately, that one deluge was the only one. Their supply was limited.

"I raced up the rough walls. Two 'demons' were waiting at the top. I dispatched one with my trusty flintlock. The other turned and ran. I quickly reloaded, then raced through the courtyard where four spearmen awaited. They waited too long. My great sword tumbled them. I ran to the heavy oaken doors of the castle itself. They were closed and barred from within. I stepped back, then hurled my weight against them. The inner wooden beam cracked and the doors flew open. Several 'demons' in the corridor turned and fled at the sight of me. I imagine I was a gruesome sight, covered with muck from the moat and blood (not my own).

"I reached heavy golden curtains over an archway. Four of the 'demons' who had fled were making a stand there, guarding what was within. As I raised my great sword, the four dropped their weapons and fell to their knees. Such cowardice was unpardonable. I pushed them aside and strode through the golden curtains. A soft voice came from within.

" 'At last, man of mystery. I have waited for you.' That was not the greeting I had expected. I entered. It was the throne room, a huge ornate place, filled with hundreds of burning candles and thousands of flowers. Seated, or perhaps half-reclining on a golden couch that served as a throne, was the most beautiful woman I had ever seen.

"I do not have the skill of a poet to properly describe her. Her hair was golden and long, her eyes large and black, her skin as fair and smooth as a flower petal or the wing of a butterfly. She was clad in a shimmering robe that seemed to reveal yet conceal the perfect ivory body beneath. As I stood there, she laughed, the silvery laughter of a young girl.

" 'What took you so long?' she said.

" 'Are you the Hanta witch?' I stammered. After the violence and gore I had gone through, I felt like a fool standing before this fantastic woman among the myriad candles and flowers.

" 'Ignorant fools call me that,' she said, frowning. 'I am the ruler of this land and my proper title is Queen.'

" 'You say you've waited for me, madam. May I inquire why?'

" 'You may. First, pray be seated.'

" 'I will stand,' I said, almost dazzled by the shimmering gown that reflected the candle flames. Again, her silvery laughter.

" 'I am not "madam," ' she continued. 'I have no husband. I am unwed. Is that clear?'

" 'Clearly stated.'

" 'That is why I waited for you,' she said with a strange smile.

" 'That is not clear,' I said.

" 'I need a husband to manage my vast properties, to guard my great treasure, to command my small army, and share my throne. I have chosen you. Now will you be seated?'

"I sat on a stool covered with a curious hide unknown to me; some species of giant snake or lizard.

" 'Chose me to wed, whom you've never seen before? Whose face you do not see now?' I said. I still wore my costume.

" 'I have seen and heard' enough,' " she said, taking a

feathery flower from a vase and wafting it gently before her nostrils. 'We watched you fight your way through my land, against animals and men, against my own demons.' She gave an odd pronunciation to the word. 'Now you are here.' She bent near me and waved the flower close to my face. The air was filled with her own perfume, a tantalizing, heady scent. I am not a man given to quivering, but I quivered then at the close proximity of this blonde witch.

" 'All the reports about you were true. I waited here, excited and anxious for your arrival. I watched you in the pass. I watched you climb the walls. I knew that if you made your way to this room, against all the odds placed upon you, the die was cast. You are here. The die is cast. You are a fit mate for the Queen of Hanta. So shall it be.'

"I took a deep breath. This dazzling creature was offering herself to me. A servant entered silently, bearing a tray with two silver goblets. He offered one to me. I took it while I gathered my thoughts. Her great shining eyes watched me.

" 'Is it Queen or witch of Hanta?' I asked.

" 'You may choose your own title,' she said, laughing.

" 'Your Highness, I did not come here to wed you, but to stop your murderous treatment of the caravans.'

" 'Are you wed? Do you have a good wife back in your jungle?' she asked.

" 'I have no wife.'

" 'So I was informed. In truth, I am a peace-loving woman, and indeed a mate worthy of you. Who is more suitable than you, ruler of the jungle? Come, drink to our troth.'

"Her face was close to mine. Her perfume and her warmth were (I can only think of one proper word here) unhinging me. I quickly drank to cover my embarrassment.

" 'I drink because I am thirsty,' I said. And that was a true statement. After the last battle, my throat was dry.

"Again, her silvery laughter.

" 'You are a rude jungle giant. I have waited for a real man like you all my life. Now that you are here.' Her lips brushed my forehead—'I cannot let you go.'

I staggered to my feet. The room swam before my eyes. The myriad candles and her shimmering gown became one vast flame. I fell to my knees.

" 'Witch, you drugged me with that foul drink,' I said as I felt hands grasping me. I tried to fight them off, but I was too weak. I lost consciousness."

The Phantom paused in his reading of the old chronicle. Even in 1675, that dope-drink trick must have been an old one. What had this Hanta woman really been? Witch or queen? One thing appeared certain. She was the leader of a murderous gang of cutthroats. But the Eighth had returned to write this history, so the answer must be here. Another drink of cold spring water, another petting for dozing Devil who opened his pale-blue eyes briefly, and he read on.

"I awoke in a dungeon, behind bars. As such places go, the cell was clean, without the usual vermin, and a board with food and drink was at the side of my cot. I was furious at having been trapped by such a simple ruse. I shook the bars and roared. The beauteous witch appeared."

The Phantom paused again. What did the word "appeared" mean? Did she come out of thin air, or reach the cell in a normal manner?

" 'Calm yourself, jungle king,' she said, and her perfume wafted through the bars to me. 'I did this only to keep you from running away. I love you. I need you.'

"She said these words with such sincerity that I almost believed her. But I remembered the pillaged caravans.

" 'Love me? You lie, witch. What of your "blood-drinking demons?" What of your attacks on peaceful caravans?'

" 'People lie. I am a woman alone here. My demons guard me. I need monies to feed my retainers and run my castle. I exact a tax from caravans, like any sovereign. And if they refuse to pay, and thus break the law of this land, they must be punished.'

" 'Tax? Witch's gold,' I said.

" 'Fool, why won't you believe me?' she cried. And she wept. But I noted that she stayed out of reach of my hands through the bars.

" 'Witch's tears,' I said.

"She choked away her tears, almost like a normal human woman, and now her eyes blazed with fury. 'You are a fool. A great ponderous fool. You will not leave this cell until you get some sense in that thick skull.'

" 'How many other great ponderous fools have you lured here to rot in these foul dungeons?' I shouted. Her eyes blazed. But she did not answer. She turned away and disappeared."

Disappeared into thin air, or merely walked away? The chronicle did not make it clear.

"I had been tricked once by this witch of Hanta. I would not be tricked again. It was time I left this cell. I picked up a goblet of wine, then called to a nearby guard. He approached the cell cautiously. He was an ordinary dull brute of a man without the demon mask.

" 'How can I drink this wine? It is foul,' I said.

" 'But I had a dram from the same jug,' he said.

" 'Foul,' I said. 'Smell for yourself.'

"The dull fellow took me at my word, and put his pimply nose near the bars. I tossed the wine quickly into his eyes, and, as he sputtered, grasped his throat in a firm grip. He then had the choice of having his neck broken, or unlocking my cell. He chose the latter. Outside, I relieved him of his sword and dagger, and left him in my place, unconscious but breathing. I moved cautiously through the subterranean corridor. A guard with a musket turned in surprise as I came up behind him. His moment of hesitation was enough. I left him on the stone floor and moved on. I stopped before a heavy oaken door that had a small barred opening. Peering in, I saw that it was an arsenal. The door was locked with a heavy rusted chain and an old metal lock. I broke the chain with a quick twist and entered the room. There were dozens of weapons, some new, some of great antiquity. I am interested in weapons and would have been happy to spend time studying them. But there was no time. From the sound of voices and running feet outside, I knew my escape had been discovered. In addition to the weapons, there were stacks of barrels filled with gunpowder, enough to blow up the entire castle. And that was my intention—to destroy this evil place. I hurriedly searched for and found fuses and flint. I smashed open several barrels and placed a fuse in the heap of black powder. Using the flints, I produced a spark that ignited the fuse. I waited a moment to be certain it was burning properly. When I was sure it was, I ran out with my great sword in one hand, a loaded pistol in the other, and three more loaded pistols in my belt. As it turned out, I had no need of these weapons.

"Several of the demons fled at the sight of me, and I had barely reached the throne room when the first explosion shook the castle. Voices howled on all sides. I rushed through the golden curtains. There she stood, her fists clenched, her eyes blazing. Behind her were the flames of the myriad candles, as thick as stars in the sky on a clear moonless night.

" 'Oh you great fool! What have you done?' she cried. There were tears in her eyes, and even as she spoke another explosion shook the floor and walls. 'Why couldn't you believe me?' Those were her last words as the ceiling shook and began to fall around us. I caught her as she fainted and rushed out with her in my arms. What else could I do? I raced across the courtyard to the outer battlements. The entire castle was rent with enormous explosions. The drawbridge was up. There was no time to lower it. Towers were crashing around us. Great fires were roaring up out of the collapsing castle. I took one last backward look. Demons were rushing blindly through the flames and smoke of the inferno. Then with the blonde witch of Hanta in my arms, I leaped from the wall to the moat far below. . ."

That was the end of the history. An abrupt ending. Also the end of that volume. There were no more pages. This was maddening. What had happened after that? The Phantom searched other volumes of the period. There was no more mention of the Witch of Hanta or of Koqania. He returned to the original volume and examined the binding. A tiny fragment of vellum remaining in the binding gave him a clue. There had been another page, maybe more than one. But it had been removed. This vellum, lamb gut prepared as parchment, was tough and fairly permanent and not easy to tear out. But why? Obviously the eighth Phantom had returned to the Skull Cave after that adventure and written here. But what had happened to the Hanta witch? Old Mozz, who had heard all and forgotten nothing, was to give him the answer.

CHAPTER 3

The castle ruins covered many acres on the mountain slope. The few travelers who reached this remote place marveled at the vast stonework, and wondered what monarch had ruled there. But the farmers and herdsmen who lived in the area knew nothing of the history, only weird legends. And at the present time, they were more loath than ever to talk about it. A closer inspection might show that there was once a mighty fire among these crumbled walls, but the winds and rains of centuries had washed away all but faint traces. Near the center of the stone heaps and partial walls, a broken stone staircase led down into the ground. It led to a rusted iron door fastened with a ponderous iron chain and an old lock. It would appear that this iron door opened onto still existing cellars of the old castle, but no one in recent times had tried to enter the place. The excuse was that it was unsafe. Ancient ceilings and walls might collapse on the foolhardy intruder. Or old pits might open under his feet. That was the excuse; the real reason was that as long as anyone could remember, there were said to be things in those dark cellars, What kind of things? Just things.

If a curious person was bold enough to climb down the broken stone stairs and reach the locked iron door, he might notice, if there was light enough, a strange mark over the door. A death's head. A mark that neither washing or scouring could remove. A mark so old it seemed to be a part of the pattern of the rough stone. What the curious person could not see was a small metal spring hidden in the iron doorframe behind the lower hinge.

On this particular dark night, a night with no moon, the heavy iron door slowly opened on its rusty, creaking hinges. This action released the hidden spring which in turn activated a tiny radio transmitter, concealed in the stone wall behind the doorframe. The transmitter broadcast an ultra-high-frequency signal, silent in the immediate area, but strong enough to travel thousands of miles. Strong enough to travel to the Skull Cave in the Deep Woods.

On the radio panel in the rocky chamber, a small red light flicked on, accompanied by a soft buzzing. Dozing on a pile of animal skins a few yards away, Devil suddenly awoke. His ears were instantly alert. His pale-blue eyes popped open, and he was on his feet in a split second. He moved quickly to the radio chamber, saw the flickering red light, then turned and ran out of the cave. The Phantom was seated on the ground near the Skull Throne, about to begin dinner. Guran, Rex, Tomm, and the boys's tutor, stylish Miss Tagama, were eating with him and Old Mozz, having tottered onto the scene, was invited to join them. The old man, his joints creaking like a wooden rocker, bowed with the grace of a courtier.

"You sent for me, O Ghost Who Walks?"

"I found the tale of the Hanta witch as you predicted," said the Phantom.

"And was it not an astonishment?" said Old Mozz.

"It was truly."

Chief Guran looked at the Phantom reproachfully.

"You said you would tell me of the astonishment," he said.

"Tell us about the witch," shouted Rex.

"Witch?" said Miss Tagama, recently returned from two years at the Sorbonne. "I hope you're not filling the boys' heads with such nonsense."

"Not nonsense," said Old Mozz angrily.

"I will not have the boys confused with this old-fashioned jungle superstition," she replied tartly.

The Phantom laughed, raising his hand for peace between the two.

'Tell us," said Rex and Tomm eagerly.

"Later. Mozz, the tale of the Hanta witch that I found in the chronicles is incomplete. How did it end?"

"Your father and his father before him asked me the same question," said Old Mozz, chuckling. His chuckle was somewhere between a wheeze and a grunt.

"They did? They read the tale too?" said the Phantom, fascinated by any mention of his forebears.

"Yes. It is an ancient matter," said Mozz.

"A page or more is missing from the chronicle."

"So they told me."

"Do you know how it ended?"

Old Mozz looked hurt.

"Do I know?" he said, as though this was the most ridiculous thing in the world to say to a man who had heard all and forgotten nothing.

"And will you tell me?"

"I will, O Ghost Who Walks."

At this moment, Devil ran out of the cave. He came directly to the Phantom and stood looking at him intently.

"What, Devil?"

As if in answer, Devil turned and walked slowly back to the cave, looking back at the Phantom as he went. The Phantom sprang to his feet and followed.

"Devil never comes to me like that without a reason," he said.

"But the witch, the Hanta witch?" cried Rex.

"In a moment," said the Phantom, entering the cave.

In the radio chamber, the red light was still flickering, the soft buzzing continuing. This seemed to surprise the Phantom. He watched it for a few moments, then checked to see if there was a short circuit. There was none. Then, as he watched, the red light went off and the buzzing stopped. There was no reason to doubt what this meant. The iron door in the distant ruins of Koqania had been opened. Then closed. Someone—something—had entered the Phantom's hideout.

He visualized the place. He had visited it once, several years ago, remembering tales about it from his father. It had always been a Phantom hideout. No one knew why. The Hanta witch. It was one of the few hideouts in Europe. (There was another in a Roman crypt and another in a Paris tower.) These hideouts were homes away from home for the Phantoms when they traveled to that part of the world. Each generation or two had added such spots, and they were now scattered around the earth in the most unlikely places.

During that visit, he had installed the spring and transmitter, and put a new lock on the door. He had used an antique lock that would not look out of place. He knew that the local people, for their own reasons, would not enter the ruins. But someone had. Now, coming after the newscasts about "the plague of vampires led by a witch in Koqania," this seemed more than a coincidence. He needed more information. He sat at his radio transmitter, turned on his private X-band, and reached Jungle Patrol headquarters in Mawitaan, the capital city of Bangalla, some five hundred miles away.

The patrolman operating the switchboard was shaken by the signal. The X-band was rarely used. When it flashed on, none of them knew where it came from, but they knew who it was: the unknown commander of the Jungle Patrol. For centuries, the commander at the top of the organization chart had always remained unknown. Nobody knew why. That is the way it was, one of the strongest and most treasured traditions of the Patrol.

The phone rang at the bedside of Colonel Worobu. Worobu was the new C.O. of the Patrol, having come up through the ranks to succeed Colonel Randolph Weeks, retired. The colonel, awakened out of a sound sleep, opened one eye and looked at the clock at his bedside. He was enjoying his nap after a heavy meal. The patrol knew better than to disturb him at this hour. Only in emergencies or when . . . it could be. *He* always called when Worobu was asleep. Didn't he ever sleep (whoever he was)? He cleared his throat and grabbed the phone.

"Colonel Worobu here."

The anticipated voice came through—big, deep, and resonant. (Where did he call from?)

"Colonel, please do the following for me." (He never wasted time with small talk such as "how are you." He always got right to the point).

"Please wire the police chief in Koqania. K-o-q-a-n-i-a. Ask him about the news reports concerning the vampires—and the witch."

"I beg your pardon, sir?"

"The Mawitaan newscast had several stories about it. Did you hear them?"

"As a matter of fact, now that you mention it, I did."

"Very good. Please let me know as soon as you have information. Thank you, Colonel." Click.

That was it. Like it always was. Quick. Right to the point. Vampires? It sounded silly. But the commander didn't waste his time. If he wanted something, there was a reason. He phoned back to his headquarters switchboard.

"Sergeant, this is Colonel Worobu. I want to send an overseas cable to the police chief in Koqania. K-o-q-a-n-i-a."

CHAPTER 4

When the Phantom returned to his dinner in the chamber of the Skull Throne, Chief Guran and the boys were pestering Old Mozz with questions about the Hanta witch. But he sat smiling and unmoved, refusing to say a word. All turned to the Phantom.

"What did Devil want?" asked Tomm.

"Who was the Hanta witch?" said Guran.

"Hey, how about the Gooley-Gooley witch?" said Rex, remembering the odd name. The Phantom smiled at them and began to eat.

"So many questions. I will tell you about the Hanta witch quickly because I have my own question to ask Mozz."

He gave them a short summary of the story he had read, skimming over the violence and ending with the jump into the moat.

"That's where the chronicle stopped. What happened next, Mozz?"

Mozz climbed laboriously to his feet. He preferred to stand when he told his tales. Of all the tellers of the jungle, he was the most admired, and as he began in his sing-song voice several dozen of the pygmy Bandar sat quietly in the shadows, listening.

"Now when the Phantom leaped from the flaming castle with the beauteous witch of Hanta in his arms, it is told that the blood-drinking demons perished in the flames."

The boys sat up at that, and Miss Tagama clicked her tongue disapprovingly. The Phantom had not mentioned *them*.

"Yet, it is possible that some survived the holocaust and roam the earth still, for, it is said, that species of demon does not perish."

"Really!" said Miss Tagama, a trim black figure in her bright sarong.

"Shh," said Rex and Tomm.

"It is said that soon after the destruction of the evil castle, there was a violent storm, as though the gods of that place were showing their wrath. And the great rains put out the fires, but after the storm there was nothing left of that place but ruins, heaps upon heaps of rock. Now the Phantom and the witch had taken shelter in a cave until the storm passed. And though she tried to ply her magic and her spells upon him"—old Mozz permitted himself to grin at that—"he was too strong and did not succumb, for she was evil, this witch of Hanta. And though she wept and pleaded, he knew what he must do. He carried her back into the ruins of that old castle, down into the caverns and chambers that remained beneath the heaps of rubble and stone. And there, deep in the earth, where none could see her, he chained her securely to a pillar of stone, for she was evil, this witch of Hanta."

"Awful," muttered Miss Tagama, who'd had some contact with Women's Lib groups in Paris.

"Shh," said the boys.

"And then"—-Old Mozz paused dramatically—"something strange and curious took place in that vault beneath the earth." He paused to take a dipper of cold spring water from a jug at his feet. He drank it slowly, looking slyly at the eager, impatient faces around him.

"What?" said Rex.

"This young witch, whose beauty had been compared to the sunrise and the flowers of the field, this beauteous young creature turned into a shriveled old hag before his very eyes."

"Because she was really old," said Tonm.

"And she shrieked and she wailed. And this withered old crone begged him to kiss her before he departed, but he wisely refused. For if he kissed her, he would restore her youth and beauty—and free her from the chains. And so he left her, shrieking and moaning. And to this day she shrieks and moans, but nothing can free her and nothing can return her to youth and beauty, nothing save the kiss of the Phantom. But that she will never receive, for she is evil, this witch of Hanta."

Rex stared at the old man, who had suddenly become silent

and motionless like a movie film that suddenly stops.

"She's still alive?" said Rex. Old Mozz did not answer. He stood like a polished statue.

"The story is over. Off to bed," said the Phantom. The boys left, after a quick kiss for Uncle Walker, then ran off chattering about the story.

"Mozz, is that the story as you heard it?" asked the Phantom.

"As it was told me."

"Who told it to you?"

"The teller who was my grandsire."

"Is there no more to the story?"

"Nothing more."

"Thank you. That was well told."

"Thank you, O Ghost Who Walks."

The Phantom was shaken by Mozz's story. Coming after the chronicle, it sounded so real. Yet it was obviously legend, myth. Not real, of course. Of course not.

CHAPTER 5

The little town huddled in the narrow valley between two mountain ranges. It was as old as the castle ruins on the nearest peak, and was made of the same gray granite. The narrow cobblestone streets had known the tread of the Crusaders a millennium earlier. Through the centuries, a dozen armies had marched through this valley and town, looting and pillaging the crops and farms, raping the women, often forcing the men into service or slavery. It is no wonder that the inhabitants were still hostile and suspicious toward strangers. In the middle of the town, a small stone building with heavy bars on some of its little windows bore a sign over the front entrance: POLICE.

The cable was delivered there. The police force in this small place consisted of two men, Chief Peta and his assistant, Sergeant Malo. Malo read the telegram and grinned. He was slim, with an olive complexion, shining black hair and a pencil-thin mustache. He entered the chief's office without knocking. As usual, the chief was dozing at his desk, his head resting on his arms as he snored. When Malo slammed the office door, the chief awoke with a start and much snorting to clear his head. He had a round face with big handlebar mustaches, shaggy gray hair, a ruddy complexion from high blood pressure, and a red nose from heavy consumption of the local schnapps. His collar was open at the throat, his jacket unbuttoned and covered with ashes from chain-smoking. He hurriedly lit a fresh cigarette and looked at Malo with bleary eyes that were bloodshot from lack of sleep.

"I told you a dozen times to knock before you come in here," he said peevishly.

The immaculate Malo looked scornfully at him. "I did," he replied, lying. "But you didn't hear me."

"Well, what is it?" The chief was obviously in a nervous state.

"A cable from overseas, from Bangalla."

The chief fumbled for his glasses, but had forgotten where he left them.

"Read it," he said brusquely.

"It says, 'Advise about accuracy of reports about vampires in your district.'"

"It says what?" stammered the chief.

"I'll read it again. 'Advise about accuracy of reports about vampires in your district.' Signed Colonel Worobu, C.O. Jungle Patrol, Mawitaan, Bangalla."

"Bangalla?" said the chief. "Where in hell is that?" Malo grinned and waved his hand to the south.

"In the tropics, a few thousand miles that way."

"Jungle Patrol, Colonel—what is all that?" said the chief thickly, his head still dizzy from the last glass of brandy.

"That's all there is," said Malo, watching the chief with scarcely concealed contempt.

"What's it to him? Tell that colonel a million miles from here that it's none of his damned business!" he blustered.

"You sure that's what I should answer, Chief?" said Malo.

"No, wait a minute."

The chief got up and walked unsteadily to a sink in the corner. He let the water run until it was cold, then drank a glassful. He stared at his bloodshot eyes in the cracked, dirty mirror, then washed his face in the cold water.

There were no towels so he dried his hands and face on a shirttail. His sleek assistant watched without comment.

"No, Malo. Tell that colonel this: the reports about the vampire, and the witch, are sheer nonsense. Got that? Sheer nonsense."

"He didn't ask about a witch," said Malo with a poker face.

The chief shook himself.

"He didn't? I thought he said—?"

"Nothing about a witch. He just asked about vampires. Evidently, the international press has sent out stupid rumors." He said the last two words slowly.

"Stupid is right, the damn busybodies. Look, I gave you the reply, didn't I?"

"The reports about vampires are sheer nonsense. Anything else?"

"No, that's enough. Go on and send it."

"Yes, sir." Malo stressed the last word more than necessary, then did a smart military about face and left the office. The chief stared after him. That Malo was efficient, but he lacked respect. The sergeant's contemptuous manner was not lost on him. Why shouldn't he be like that? the chief thought. I'm not worth respecting. I'm a coward. He went to the window, one of the few without bars in this stationhouse that also served as a jail. Outside, daylight was fading, the shadows deepening. He shuddered, shut the window, and returned to his desk.

"Sheer nonsense. Sheer nonsense," he muttered to himself. "How I wish it was."

He opened the bottom drawer of his desk, took out the jug of brandy, filled the water glass, and gulped it down.

CHAPTER 6

Nighttime had become frightening in Koqania, because of the rumors and the stories and the strange sounds in the dark, and not many left their houses after sunset. But daytime was like any other country place, with flowers and birds, men working in the fields, and children singing and gathering flowers on their way to school. There weren't as many children now, because some families had moved away, and on this dirt road there were deserted farms. The girls were skipping and the boys playing leapfrog, when they found the man lying in the ditch. At first, they thought he was asleep or drunk. He was neither. He wouldn't wake up. They began to scream and ran across the field where two men were mowing hay. The men came to the ditch while the children kept a safe distance. One of the girls was hysterical. She had seen the fallen man's face.

The dead man was a local farmer both men knew. They were not unfamiliar with death. In this remote place, people prepared their own dead for burial. But the sight of this corpse terrified them. They did not scream as the children had, but they ran as fast as they could toward the town and the police station. The dead man's throat had been torn.

In the Skull Cave, a bell rang in the radio panel. The

Phantom was nearby in his major treasure room where he had been polishing Excalibur, earlier known as Caledwoolch, the sword of King Arthur. He put on the earphones.

"Colonel Worobu here. Do you receive me?" said the voice.

"I receive you, Colonel."

"I have the reply from Koqania which reads as follows. Quote: 'The news reports of Vampires here are sheer nonsense. Repeat sheer nonsense.' End quote. Signed Ivor Peta, Police Chief, Koqania. Sounds like he means it," added Worobu with a chuckle.

"Yes it does, Colonel. Thank you."

"Anything else?"

"Not now. Good night."

In his office, Worobu stared at his telephone which was hooked up to the Patrol transmitter.

"Now what was that all about?" he asked aloud. He hung up the receiver and looked quickly about the room. He was alone. It wouldn't do to be seen talking to one's self. Might look peculiar. But what was that all about?

Moments later, the Phantom tuned in the Mawitaan news broadcast to hear the following: "Here's another odd report from that faraway place called Koqania that seems to continue to live in the sixteenth century. A murder case. A man was found dead; the farmers say he was killed by a vampire. No mention of a witch this time. Maybe it was her night off. Sounds like a nice little spot, Koqania, in case you're looking for a quiet vacation." The announcer, Seguno Togando, had made a reputation as a wit, and people enjoyed his humorous newscasts.

The news reports went on in a more serious vein. Trouble in the Orient. Oil shortages. Strikes everywhere. The Phantom half-listened, wondering about what he had heard. At that moment, the little red pilot light flicked on and the soft buzzer sounded. Once again, something had opened the iron door to the castle ruins in Koqania.

He stared at the tiny flickering light. This time the coincidence of the report from Worobu, the newscast, and this signal was too meaningful to ignore. He sat for a moment as motionless as a statue. Then he turned off the radio panel and strode out of the cave. For the Phantom, to think was to act. His life had often depended on split-second decisions. It had become a habit. As he passed the rocky chamber of the Phantom Chronicles, he glanced at the volume still on the podium, the volume with the missing last page. Something was going on in Koqania, something that somehow, someway, involved that three-hundred-year-old tale.

As he reached the cave mouth, Rex and Tomm were sitting with Devil and Miss Tagama. The boy sprang up, jumping into the

Phantom's arms.

"I must go away for a while, Rex."

"Is it about the vampires?" asked the boy excitedly.

"How did you know that?"

"I could hear the radio."

"Yes, it's about that."

"But you said vampires are not real."

"So I did, and so they are not. They are imaginary like fairies or goblins."

"But I saw a goblin the other day."

"Now, Rex," said the Phantom, laughing.

"Didn't we see a goblin by the stream, Tomm? Didn't we?" Rex's black friend nodded solemnly.

The Phantom laughed and moved with his friends to the corral where he hurriedly saddled his great white stallion, Hero. Sharing the corral with Hero were two of Rex's pets, Kateena, the lioness, and Joomba, the elephant. Rex sat on Kateena's back, watching the saddling of Hero.

"Uncle Walker, please take me along."

"And have you miss school? How about that, Miss Tagama?"

The pretty tutor in her flaming sarong laughed and shook her head. "He has enough trouble keeping up when he's here."

"Sorry, Rex."

The boy ran to him excitedly. "I'll take my books. I'll study every day. I'll do my homework. Honest I will." The Phantom lifted him in his arms and kissed him, then put him down. "No, Rex. There might be some problems on this trip."

"You mean danger?"

"Problems. Good-bye all."

"Uncle Walker, you forgot. You promised to tell us about that other witch—the Gooley-Gooley witch," said Rex, trying to delay the inevitable departure.

"I promised no such thing."

"Didn't he? Didn't he?" persisted Rex to Tomm. Tomm grinned and shrugged. The Phantom motioned to Old Mozz who stood near with Chief Guran.

"Ask Old Mozz to tell you."

He swung into the saddle and, with a wave of his hand, sped off with Devil in pursuit. Rex, Tomm, Miss Tagama, Old Mozz, and Guran waved and called their good-byes. He always left like this— no luggage, no preparation. He just went. He might be gone a day or a month. Horse, rider, and wolf raced into the waterfall, one of the secret entrances to the Deep Woods, and were gone.

The great stallion sped like the wind over secret paths known only to the Bandar and the Phantom, for this was the forbidden land of the pygmy poison people. When he reached the Western jungle, inhabited by the Wambesi and Llongo, he avoided the traveled roads and villages, remaining deep in the woods. He rode for a day and a night and another day, and stopped only to water, feed, and rest his animals, taking quick catnaps for himself during these times. A few jungle folk saw him from a distance only as a blur, so fast did Hero run. And they heard the pounding of the mighty hoofs like summer thunder. This was a tale to tell their children and grandchildren, for the Phantom was rarely seen even by those jungle folk who hailed him as the Keeper of the Peace.

At the edge of the jungle, he reached a small corral hidden behind high thorn bushes. A boy wearing shorts and sneakers was waiting. He took charge of Hero, removing his bridle and saddle, and brushed the big stallion with loving hands. The boy was Tora. He lived nearby with his father, a farmer who also tended the Phantom's homing pigeons and sometimes the Phantom's fierce falcon, Fraka. Pigeons and falcon were sometimes used to carry messages to the Deep Woods.

From a chest in the shed, the Phantom took clothes— trousers, topcoat, scarf, hat, sunglasses—all of which effectively concealed his skintight costume. Then bidding Tora and Hero farewell, he walked with Devil along the path that led to the city of Mawitaan.

There are times, it is said, when the Phantom leaves the jungle and enters the town as an ordinary man. This was one of those times.

Before the big plane took off from the Mawitaan airport, there was a bit of a commotion at the bottom of the stairs. The big man wearing sunglasses was standing there with his dog, or whatever it was, on a leash. The pretty red-haired stewardess was trying to convince the big man that the animal could not go on the plane with him, even if he had bought an extra seat. She called the airline agent, a dapper fellow in a spruce blue uniform. He smiled patronizingly and explained it was against regulations. The big man asked to see the regulations. The agent took out the rule book and showed it to him in black and white— no dogs were permitted in the passenger section.

"He's not a dog. He's a wolf," said the big man. The agent and the pretty stewardesses (several of them had now gathered at the stairs) looked at the large animal in alarm. His white teeth were enormous and his eyes were pale blue. The agent backed off a step or two, and pointed out another regulation: no wild animals permitted aboard.

"He's not wild. He's tame and trained," said the big man patiently. "Do you have a rule about a tame wolf?"

"Not exactly. But sir, the rule covers all pets."

"He is not a pet. He is a working animal. He works for me."

"But sir," said the agent.

Now, after a brief silence, the big man seemed to grow a foot taller, and his pleasant voice became cold.

"I cannot trust this wolf to your freight section. The air pressure and temperature are not adjusted properly. At thirty-thousand feet, he would be permanently injured or killed. He is well behaved and will bother no one. He will board with me."

The stewardess looked at the agent, who was sweating and red-faced. They waited to hear him say no. But he didn't. He stared at the dark sunglasses as though hypnotized.

"I cannot be responsible," he stammered.

"The responsibility is mine," said the big man. And he went up the stairs with the animal on the leash. The agent breathed deeply.

"You let him do it?" said the red-haired stewardess, amazed.

He scowled and turned away.

"Get ready to take off," he snapped, and went back to the office.

"How about that?" said the redhead.

"There are some men you don't say no to. That's one of them."

The girls laughed. The brunette looked up at the open cabin door.

"I wish I was going on this flight. I wonder who he is."

"Passenger list says 'Mr. Walker and friend,'" said the redhead. "How about that friend?"

"Mr. Walker. We'll find out more about him on the flight," said the blonde.

When the plane took off, the two girls almost stepped on each other trying to get to him first. He sat wearing the hat and coat.

"Can we take your hat and coat?" said the blonde.

"No, thank you," said Mr. Walker.

"You want to wear it all night?" said the redhead, giggling.

"Yes," said Mr. Walker.

The big wolf, sitting next to him, opened his mouth to yawn. The long white fangs gleamed. The girls quickly went about their business.

"What is he? Some kind of kook?" said the redhead.

"He's different," sighed the blonde.

When dinner was being served, the girls approached him

cautiously.

"We've chicken for dinner. Eh, maybe we can find him a hamburger," said the blonde. Sitting on the seat, the wolf was as tall as a man. All the passengers had taken turns walking by to see him, and they talked about him for hours. A wolf!

"He's been fed," said the big man.

"I'll bet he'd love a raw hamburger," said the blonde.

"In a pinch, yes. He prefers to kill his own meat."

The girls retreated hastily and passed the word onto the fascinated passengers and crew. He prefers to kill his own meat!

When the big man and his "friend" left the plane at Rome after the long flight, the girls had learned nothing more about him. Only his name, Mr. Walker, which sounded ordinary enough. They might have found it less ordinary if they knew what it stood for— the Ghost Who Walks.

He left Rome by rail, and changed trains three times before reaching the tiny station at Koqania. He was the only passenger to get off the train. It was twilight and the stone station was locked. The platform and area about the building were deserted and unlit. Neither mailbags nor parcels were left by the train. He had barely descended the steps with Devil when the train chugged off as though anxious to get away. The lone conductor had looked at him in surprise when he had seen his ticket marked for Koqania. Now as the single dusty old coach car passed, the conductor peered at him from a window, still looking surprised. Obviously, traffic for Koqania was sparse.

He looked around. The small town was a few hundred yards away. Pale light glimmered through cracks in a few windows. The street was not completely deserted. A carriage and horse, with a driver wearing a top hat, stood a block away. The Phantom walked to him with Devil on his leash. The driver was an elderly man with big gray mustaches. He looked with some amazement at the Phantom.

"I always park down here to watch the train. Three times a week it goes by. The only excitement in town," he said, chuckling. "But its been a long time since anybody got off."

"Is there a taxi here?"

"I'm the taxi."

"Are you available?"

The old man snorted. "I haven't had any business for a month. Used to have plenty. But who wants a taxi here these days?"

The Phantom climbed into the carriage.

"Where to, sir? The inn?" said the old man, suddenly

professional. He chuckled. "It's not far. You could walk."

"Can you take me to the castle?"

The old man turned in his seat and looked at the Phantom.

"The castle?" he said, his eyes wide.

"Is there more than one?"

"You mean—the castle ruins?"

"Yes."

"You sure you want to go there."

"Yes."

"It's almost dark. That's it up there." He pointed ahead. A mile or more away, the broken battlements of the castle loomed in the dusk.

"Okay, let's go."

"Mister, I'll take you there, but I want to get home by dark. It'll be close."

"Right. Get going."

The carriage rattled over the old cobblestones as they raced through the town as fast as the old mare could pull them. A few people were on the sidewalks, entering their houses. They looked curiously at the carriage. He noticed that most of the windows were already covered with shutters and the remainder were being shut as he rolled by.

They were outside the town in a few minutes, rolling along a rough dirt road. The carriage stopped by an open field a quarter of a mile from the base of the peak. The ruins could be seen vaguely in the gathering darkness.

"This is as far as I go," said the old man.

The Phantom jumped out of the carriage with Devil and offered him money.

"That money's no good here."

"I haven't had a chance to get your Koqania money."

"Pay me tomorrow. I'm easy to find," said the driver, anxious to be off.

"You don't want to wait here until I come back?"

"Come back? You going up there?" said the old man, appalled.

"Yes."

"Mister, you're a stranger. Don't you know about this place?"

"No. Tell me."

"You can't go up there night or day, especially night. You can't stay out here on this road. You better come back with me."

As he spoke, the driver was wheeling horse and carriage about to return to town. In his hurry, his carriage almost rolled into a ditch.

"It's a quiet lovely night. Why can't I be there? Or go there?"

"Because she is there. And they are there. And here."

"Who?"

"The vampires, and the witch." He almost hissed the words softly, as though afraid someone else might hear.

"Have you seen them?"

"Not me."

"Who has?"

"Plenty have. Look, mister, it's almost dark. I can't sit out here arguing with you. I warned you." He raised his long whip and lashed the mare. The old horse took off with a start. The Phantom watched for a moment, then walked into the field with Devil. He removed the leash, and man and wolf began to walk toward the ruins. The driver looked back as he bounced away.

"The fool," he said. "The crazy fool! I wonder who he was."

CHAPTER 7

A gibbous moon, between half and full, moved in and out of heavy clouds as he walked up the slope. Devil roamed through the high grass a few yards ahead of him. As he climbed the incline which became steeper as he neared the ruins, he thought about his ancestor, the eighth Phantom. Here is where he had battled with the "blood drinking demons" and "the gargoyles of the witch of Hanta" three centuries ago. Soon he reached a bank. Below was a deep ditch filled with water, weeds, and water plants. The old moat! Here the eighth Phantom had fought "creepy things, some with tentacles." Boiling lead had fallen into it, perhaps leaving traces that could still be found. He walked along the bank and reached a place where tons of stone had tumbled into the moat, probably at the time of that old explosion. This provided a bridge across the moat. Now he came to broken walls and heaps of stone, the ancient battlements of the castle. From above here, the eighth Phantom had leaped into the moat with the "beauteous blonde witch" in his arms. To be in this place after reading that tale in the chronicles was like reliving a dream.

He moved quietly among the ruins with Devil, pausing now and then to test the air for sounds, Devil testing for scents. Nothing suspicious. And nothing appeared changed from his last visit here several years before. He found the old stone staircase and climbed down to the iron door. Standing in the dark, he snapped on a small but powerful flashlight. The old lock was in place on the door as he had left it. Above the door was the faint skull mark left by an earlier Phantom visitor. It was from this door, on being opened, that a radio signal had been sent all the way to the Skull Cave. But the door was locked. Had the hidden transmitter malfunctioned, sending a false alarm? He examined the lock under the light beam. The dust on it was not evenly distributed. It had been touched, disturbed. And there were faint scratches around the keyhole. Someone had opened it with an instrument, or a skeleton key. He unlocked it, opened the door. The rusty old hinges creaked as they always had. He touched the hidden spring, turning it off, then entered the dark tunnel with Devil. His light beam was off, and he walked softly in the dark, as softly as Devil. ("The Phantom moves on cat's feet" was an old jungle saying.)

He was moving through a rocky cellar corridor that led to a maze of tunnels under the ruins. Here and there ceilings had caved in, but most of the ancient chambers, some large, some tiny, were intact.

He paused at one heavy oaken door, and turning on the flashlight, peered in. This was a small cell with a barred window that let in air and light in the daytime. It opened on an airshaft. In the small chamber were a cot, table, candles. On these rare occasions when a Phantom slept in the ruins, this was the place. Why here? Of all the countless chambers, some airier and more usable, why this one? Was it for sentimental reasons? Was this the dungeon where the eighth Phantom had been imprisoned by the witch? It could be. He was suddenly certain. It must be. The heavy door had the small barred opening described in the chronicle. He could picture the blonde witch peering in, her eyes filled with "witch's tears." He closed the door and moved on. Devil was sniffing in the dark. He snapped on his beam. A torch made of oil-soaked reeds was stuck in a socket on the wall. It had recently been lit and some of the oil had dripped to the floor.

Now he moved more cautiously. The corridor opened into a large chamber that he remembered. He snapped on his light Yes, all the old paraphernalia was still there, rusted and decaying, but still recognizable. This had been an ancient torture chamber.

There was a pit where fires had been built to heat pincers and other instruments red-hot. There was a rack used to stretch victims until bones were pulled from sockets. A gallows. A metal "shoe" with a screw device. And weirdest of all, the "Iron Maiden." This was a large empty form of metal shaped like a woman wearing long skirts. It opened on hinges. The inside surface was lined with sharp spikes. The victim was placed inside, the two halves closed, and the metal spikes penetrated non-vital areas, so that the victim died slowly. And much more. The big rocky chamber was like a museum of medieval torture instruments. But this was no museum. These thing had been used—here. And some were neither rusty nor decayed. Some were clean, oiled, recently used. Something in a corner caught his eye. A big box. He turned the beam on it. It was a coffin.

He walked to it. He did not remember its being there when he visited this place before. The coffin was not old. It was new. He opened the lid. Inside was the usual satin lining, nothing else. He touched the lining. Though these cellars were cool and damp, the lining was warm. Someone, something, had been in there and very recently. It was dark outside when the vampire roamed. He meditated for a moment. Then Devil growled.

He snapped off his light, and dropped quickly to his knees. But there was no shot in the dark. A slight scraping sound off somewhere. Then complete silence again, the silence of the tomb. Devil must have heard a rat. He shut the lid and walked back to the iron door. Outside, he closed the lock. What was going on here? Something. He had come a long way to find out. He walked out of the ruins, across the moat, and down the slope with Devil roaming a few yards ahead as before. And if there were shadows moving among the broken walls, they might have been caused by the moonlight filtering through breaks in. the clouds.

He walked on the rough dirt road that led back to town, and passed several farmhouses set back from the road. They showed no lights. Windows and doors were boarded up or open and dark. He walked to one house and looked in through the open door which was banging in the wind. He shone his flashlight into the place. It was empty, stripped of all furniture. He noticed a big barn in the back, and rows of neat well-kept fences. It looked like a successful farm. Where had the people and animals gone? Why? Two more houses on the road were similarly deserted. In one farmhouse, atop a small hill, light shone through closed shutters. He was about to knock on that door to get answers to his questions, when a horse and wagon came from a side road. A man with a lighted lantern and a rifle walked ahead of the horse. A woman holding a baby was seated on the wagon which was piled high with boxes, rolls, and furniture. As Devil ran up to the horse, the man raised his rifle.

"Don't shoot," called the Phantom. He stepped out of the driveway onto the road.

"Stay where you are," called the man.

"What is it, Miron?" asked the woman in a shrill, nervous

voice.

"I don't know."

"I'm a stranger here, a visitor," said the Phantom. "Is this the way you treat people you meet on the road, point a gun at them?"

The man held the lantern up so that the pale beam reached the Phantom's face. The man was not too reassured by this sight of a stranger wearing sunglasses on this dark night.

"Who are you?" he said, his rifle pointed at the Phantom.

"I told you. A visitor. I came to find out why people are so frightened here."

"What's he saying, Miron?"

"He says he's a visitor. He wants to know why we are so frightened. Get that animal away from me."

Devil was sniffing near him, watching the rifle. Devil knew what a rifle was. At a word from his master, he would take man and rifle to the ground. But the word didn't come.

"Here, Devil."

"What are you doing on this road at night?" said the man.

"I'm looking for vampires."

The answer caught the man by surprise. He made an odd sound, half a chuckle, half a snort.

"What did he say, Miron?"

"He said he's looking for vampires." He had trouble saying the word.

"Don't listen to him. It's a trick," shouted the woman.

"It's no trick. I just went into the ruins," said the Phantom, pointing to the distant peak.

"You went there?"

"I told you I did."

"What did you see?"

"Rocks. Nothing more."

"Are you some kind of police?"

"Umm. Yes, some kind," said the Phantom. A little white lie might reassure this frightened couple.

"He's a foreign policeman," said the man to his wife.

"Oh, that's good, that's good," she said sighing.

"We were afraid you were one of them."

"Them?"

"What you said."

"Vampires?"

"Yes." Again, the evident fear to even say the name.

"Have you ever seen one?"

"We heard some the last few nights, moaning outside the house," said the man.

"They moaned and they scratched on the walls and the

shutters," cried the woman. "I couldn't stand one more night in that place."

"She wouldn't stay the night," said the husband. "We spent all day packing. We sold our animals and fowl."

"To whom?"

The man pointed to the one lighted house the Phantom had seen.

"To that old stubborn fool. He won't leave. He'll stay until they kill him like they did Piotr and Raimond."

"What's that stubborn fool's name?"

"Roko, my second cousin. Cheated me on my animals and fowl. But who else could I sell them to?"

"Miron, let's go. I'm cold," called the wife.

"Wait. Did you sell your farm too?"

"Sell?" In spite of his fear, the man snorted angrily. "Practically gave it away."

"To your second cousin Roko?"

"Miron, stop that talking. I want to go—right now!"

"Sorry. Got to go. She's upset, leaving everything we had and so late at night. But we couldn't get packed sooner."

"What about the witch."

The man's hand shook so that he almost dropped the lantern. "Shh—don't talk about her—not here. She hears everything."

"Miron!"

"Yes, we're going. Come, Betta."

He clicked his tongue and the old mare started to move. Utensils and furniture clanked and creaked as the big old wagon rolled in the ruts.

"Who did he say he was, Miron?"

"Some kind of police."

"You know what I thought at first?"

"I know."

The voices were fainter now as the wagon rolled around a curve, out of sight. He watched them go. He knew more now than before meeting them. The vampires and the witch were not a vague story to these people. They were something real that scared them enough to make them sacrifice their life's savings and flee. He looked at the dimly lighted farmhouse. Second cousin Roko? Maybe he could tell more. But Roko could wait. Maybe there was more to be learned in town. He began to walk rapidly in the dark night, for the moon was completely covered by clouds now.

CHAPTER 8

The streets were deserted now and there were no streetlights. All the windows were shuttered. A little light came through the cracks. A pale-blue light shone over the entrance to one low building. Police. That was for later. As he walked, he saw light from an uncovered cellar window. He looked in. Men were seated about drinking. It was the local tavern and appeared to be the only nightspot in town. He went down three steps, opened the door, and entered. Devil moved in ahead of him. Every head in the place, a dozen or so in all, turned to look at him. Conversation stopped. A stout bald man wearing an apron faced him—the proprietor.

"Can I get water for my animal and milk for myself?" said the Phantom.

Someone chuckled. There were a few whispers.

"Water for your animal?" said the proprietor. He was big, with heavy arms, a thick neck, and large paunch. "This isn't a stable."

Two men seated at the wall laughed aloud at that. One was Sergeant Malo, the dapper policeman. The other one was an elegant looking gray-haired man wearing an expensive suit and a smart gray derby. He took a monocle from a breast pocket and, placing it at his eye, examined the newcomer with amazement. The Phantom looked around thoughtfully. He didn't want trouble. He wanted information.

"I'm sorry," he said. "I'm a stranger here. I didn't know where else to go."

"That's the truth," said a familiar voice. It was the old cabdriver sitting in a corner with a large mug of beer. "I drove him from the train to the castle."

That information produced a silence that was louder than words. All stared at the stranger. The castle was obviously no laughing matter. Sergeant Malo stood up.

"You went to the castle?" he asked, his voice hard.

The Phantom observed his uniform. Police. He laughed. "Yes, and was that a mistake. I read about it in the guidebooks—a landmark. I never should have let you leave me there."

"Why not?" said Sergeant Malo. "What did you see?"

"See? Nothing. It just looked spooky. I turned around and ran all the way back. I'm still out of breath."

Sergeant Malo looked at his elegant companion. Both laughed. He sat down. The others laughed. The proprietor shrugged, disappointed that the mood had changed. He had hoped for a fight, a chance to knock the stranger down. He had nothing against this particular stranger. He disliked all strangers and enjoyed knocking men down, strangers or not. He brought a bowl of water for Devil.

"No milk," he said flatly. The Phantom shrugged and sat next to the old cabdriver.

"Ran all the way back," the old man said, chuckling. "Didn't I warn you?"

"You did," said the Phantom.

Sergeant Malo and his elegant friend went to the door. The latter walked erectly with a ramrod spine that betrayed a military background. The policeman looked back at the Phantom.

"Drop by the station tonight before you go to bed. We like to know what strangers are doing here."

"Thank you," said the Phantom. "I will." He had planned to go to the stationhouse from here. The two men left.

"Did you go up to the ruins?" asked the cabby.

The others stopped talking to listen.

"Not me. It was too far, too scary."

Men around the room nodded and went back to their private conversations.

"Why is everyone selling their farms?" the Phantom asked softly.

The cabby looked about, then whispered, "You know. Out there."

The Phantom nodded. "But who's buying them?"

The proprietor went by in response to a shouted order and glared at the cabby. The old man busied himself with his drink. When he was gone, the Phantom repeated his question.

"Shh," said the cabby.

"What about the witch? Ever seen her?" said the Phantom softly. The old man looked about fearfully.

"Not me. Two kids did—the kids of poor Piotr's widow. One day—" He stopped abruptly as the proprietor strode toward them.

"We don't like strangers coming around asking questions," he said angrily. Others in the place stopped talking and watched. They did not appear surprised by their host's sudden display of bad temper. Evidently, it was a common thing.

"This is a public house," said the Phantom quietly. "You are licensed to serve food and drink, not to monitor conversation." The big man's eyes blazed. No one talked back to him. He reached down and grabbed the Phantom by the coat collar to pull him up.

"Get out!" he roared.

The words were hardly out of his mouth, when the Phantom's fist reached his jaw. It sounded like an ax hitting a tree trunk. The big man started to fall back. But the Phantom grabbed him before he fell. Then, to the amazement of the watchers, he lifted the huge man like a sack of potatoes and hurled him through the air. He crashed against the wall and fell to the floor, where he lay without moving. The Phantom started forward, the long-controlled jungle instincts in him blazing. But he stopped, trembling with the effort. The fat proprietor would never know how close he came to death that night.

The Phantom looked carefully about. Men around the room avoided the gaze behind the sunglasses. Not trusting himself to speak, he strode out quickly. The big gray wolf trotted after him. On the floor, the fat man whimpered. The drinkers breathed their relief, then turned to the cabby. Who was his friend? The cabby shook his head. Just a tourist. Like the others, he had been stunned by the fantastic power of the stranger.

Outside, the Phantom leaned against a wall to catch his breath. In his own way, he was ashamed of himself for almost losing control. As a twelve-year-old coming out of the jungle to civilization, he had had a hard lesson to learn. In his jungle, fights were rare. When you were forced into one, you fought for your life. You fought to the death. In this outer world of "civilized" men, fights were usually settled by less drastic means, except in the case of war when the jungle's way of fighting to the death was acceptable.

CHAPTER 9

Sergeant Malo looked up from his desk and was so startled his cigarette dropped from his lips. The big stranger with the sunglasses was standing at the desk looking at him. At his side was the big gray dog. It was about fifteen feet from the desk to the outside door. Malo hadn't heard him come in. He smashed out the fallen cigarette and lit a fresh one to cover his surprise.

"I came to see the chief," said the stranger.

"You came because I told you to," said Malo with a sneer.

"Have it your own way. I want to see the chief."

"What for?"

"Information."

"Who are you?"

"Name is Walker."

Malo sat back in his swivel chair. He wore a gunbelt with an automatic pistol in the leather holster. His fingers played with the holster.

"They phoned me from the tavern. You started a fight there after I left."

"No. Self-defense. A dozen witnesses."

"We don't like troublemakers in this town."

"That's natural. No town does."

"What are you doing here?"

"Tourist."

"Tourists don't come here. You're not welcome. There's a train tomorrow. Be on it."

"I've broken no law."

"We don't like nosy troublemakers."

"Nosy?"

"Prowling around. What were you doing up at the castle?"

"Sightseeing."

"You were trespassing. That's private property."

"Who owns it?"

"Absentee landlord."

The Phantom grinned. The old ruins were worthless, but had been the property of the Phantom for generations.

"We're wasting time. I'd like to talk to the chief." He moved to an office door at the side on which was lettered: CHIEF OF POLICE. The door was slightly ajar. Inside, the chief could be seen seated at his desk, head on his arms, sleeping. Malo rushed to the door and slammed it shut.

"He's busy," he snarled.

"I'll wait," said the Phantom, walking to a bench. Sergeant Malo drew his gun. The Phantom looked at him in surprise. Devil watched tensely, his pale-blue eyes fixed on the weapon.

"I told you to get out. Now you leave this town in one hour, or get locked up."

"On what charge, Sergeant?" said the Phantom quietly.

"Creating a disturbance in a public place, attacking a local citizen, and trespassing on private property. We can think of a few more if necessary," said Malo with a snarl.

"I'm sure of that. Thank you, Sergeant Malo."

The Phantom turned and left the office with Devil. Malo watched him go, then grinned. He scared easily, he told himself. Forgot he wanted to see the chief, forgot fast. He returned to his desk, replaced his gun, and reached for the phone.

The Phantom walked to the side of the building and looked in the lighted window. Inside, the chief could be seen, asleep as before. The window was closed and locked. The Phantom knocked softly on the glass pane. No reaction from the sleeping man. He knocked louder. Still no reaction. He looked closely at the window. It was locked midway up with an ordinary window latch. He put his fingers at the ledge beneath the latch and pushed up sharply, tearing the latch out of the wood frame. He hurriedly raised the window and leaped in.

The noise awakened the sleeping chief and he stared at the figure climbing in through the window, an incredible sight! Who would break into a stationhouse, into the office of the chief of police, when the latter was at his desk? The chief hurriedly took a gun from his desk's top drawer as the stranger walked to him. The chief belched and swayed as he spoke, half-drunk with brandy. The empty jug was visible in his wastebasket.

"Who—what—?" he started to say.

"Chief Ivor Peta, I've come to ask you about the vampires in this place," said the stranger.

The chief stared, his hand wavering. All he had heard about lately were vampires. This big figure in the dark glasses, was he one? The gun waved in his hand as he belched again. The stranger's hand moved faster than the chief could see. His gun was knocked out of his grip into the air, where the stranger caught it. The chief collapsed in his chair, staring with frightened eyes at the big man.

"Are you—are you—?" he stammered. The Phantom laughed.

"I'm not a vampire. I've come to ask you about them. What's the story, Chief? Do they exist or don't they?"

The stranger's laughter reassured Ivor Peta. One didn't expect a vampire to laugh, not pleasantly like that. His question was logical too. In the chief's boozy condition, it seemed proper for a stranger to break into his office and ask such a question. Besides, he was anxious to tell someone.

"It's true," said Peta. "Every word. I saw them."

The stranger sat on the edge of the desk with the gun.

"Tell me about it."

In the outer office, Sergeant Malo heard the window latch break. He drew his gun and started to rush into the inner office, then paused instead to listen at the door.

"What did you want to know?" said the chief after a moment.

"About the vampires—the plague of vampires we've heard about in the news. Are they real?"

"Are they real?" said the chief, his eyes staring. "You can believe me they're real. I saw them two nights ago."

"Tell me," said the Phantom.

'There are real vampires and bullets can't kill them," said Ivor Peta, rocking nervously in his swivel chair.

"How do you know bullets can't kill them?"

"Because I shot one, five times, with that gun!" said the chief pointing at the pistol in the Phantom's hand.

"Tell me about it."

"Two nights ago—no, three nights ago, Wednesday—I was driving on the old castle road. It was dark, at night. I saw someone ahead in my carlights, a man kneeling over something in the road. I stopped. The man was all in black with a big black hat. He was bent over a farmer. I couldn't see who it was, but I did see the muddy boots. The one in black turned to me, and I saw his face in my headlights. I had stepped out of the car by then. I saw his face."

The chief rocked in his chair at the memory and reached for a jug. But it was empty, in the wastebasket.

"Go on. Chief. You saw his face. What did it look like?"

"Awful, Horrible. Very white, as white as this paper. With long, long teeth and blood on his mouth. He had a black cloth over his eyes—like a mask and had a long knife in one hand. He started to come for me. I fired at him. He laughed. I fired again. He laughed again and kept coming. I fired five shots. I know because I counted them later. Only one bullet was left in that gun. It's still there."

The Phantom turned the cylinder and examined the bullet. He studied it a moment, then looked at the chief.

"Go on. Then what?"

"Where was I?"

"You fired five shots."

"The thing kept laughing—horrible sounds!—and kept coming at me."

"What did you do?"

"What would you do? I turned around and ran. I left my car there, just ran as fast as I could. I can still hear it laughing."

Ivor Peta sat back, exhausted by his tale.

"Did you go back the next day?"

"Yes. My car was still there. Some school children found the body. He was a cousin of mine, Piotr." The chief's voice faded. He seemed beaten, hopeless.

"What about the witch?"

The chief gasped. That question seemed more than he could handle. His mouth opened, but nothing came out.

"The witch? Did you ever see her?"

The chief looked around nervously, then answered in a whisper, as if fearing to be overheard.

"Not me. Raimond did."

"Raimond? Where is he?"

"Dead. They did it because he saw her."

"Saw her. Where?"

"Where she's always been—down there," he whispered.

"Down where?"

At that moment, Sergeant Malo burst in, gun in hand, shouting, "I told you to get out of town!"

"Chief, tell this nuisance to get lost," said the Phantom.

The chief looked at them in bewilderment.

"He's a troublemaker, a trespasser," insisted Sergeant Malo.

"Chief, I've broken no laws."

"Malo knows the law," mumbled the chief, confused.

"Broke no laws?" shouted Malo. "I charge you with breaking and entering the office of the chief of police. Look, that lock is broken."

Malo was in a rage. He quivered and his eyes were wild as he pointed the gun at the Phantom.

"We hate to shoot strangers in this town, but sometimes it is necessary for the public good!" he shouted.

"You intend to shoot me like this in cold blood?" said the Phantom slowly and clearly so the chief would hear.

"Aren't you overreacting, Sergeant Malo?"

The chief half-rose in his chair, his face ashen. "No, Malo," he cried.

"I warned you," continued Malo ignoring the chief. "Breaking in here, assaulting our chief."

"No, he didn't Malo!" shouted the chief.

"No? He's got your gun."

The Phantom had placed the gun on the desk. And as Malo pointed his gun and tensed himself to fire, the Phantom made a slight clicking noise. Devil leaped from the side. At the same time, the Phantom dropped to one knee. The wolf caught Malo by the wrist. The gun fired into the ceiling, Devil dropped back as the Phantom moved in. His fist caught Malo on the jaw. It was a hard blow. Malo flipped backward and landed in the corner, where he lay still.

"That's a bad one. You need a new helper," said the Phantom. Even this violence had not sobered up the chief. He saw it all in a haze.

"Did you kill Malo?"

"No. Not yet. I can't promise anything next time. He tried to kill me in cold blood. That needs looking into, as do your vampires. Be seeing you, Ivor Peta."

The chief shook himself and stared. Malo was still in the corner. The window was open. But the stranger and the big dog were gone. Chief Peta staggered toward Malo and bent over him . . . still breathing, jaw swelling, looked like a fracture. What a wallop! And what was that mark on the jaw? Looked like a skull, a death's head. Hadn't been there before. He staggered back to his desk and went frantically through the drawers, looking for a jug of brandy. It was all too much. He needed a drink. There were no more jugs. He grabbed the empty one out of the wastebasket and tilted it to his lips. There were a few drops left. Malo moaned in the corner. It would be several hours before he came to. *Never threaten the Phantom*— an old jungle saying.

CHAPTER 10

The Phantom and Devil rested for several hours that night in a deserted barn. The police, boozy Chief Peta and nasty Sergeant Malo, would be after him now, so that his daylight movements would be restricted. As he lay on the clean straw, he considered what his detective work had turned up so far. Several murders had been committed by persons unknown, believed by these people to be vampires. (Descendants of the "blood-drinking demons" or the same eternal ones?) Several witnesses had either heard or seen these vampires, including Chief Peta himself. Five shots. The Phantom thought about this for a moment. Curious, but an interesting lead.

And the witch. Everyone seemed afraid even to talk about her. The farmer, the cabby, and the chief all acted as though she could overhear them wherever they were. A man named Raimond had seen her and, because of that, had been killed by them (the vampires?), presumably at her command. And the children had seen her, the children of Piotr's widow. Piotr had been the chiefs second cousin, the one killed on the road the night of the five shots. The children had seen her, but where? "Down there where she always was," according to Chief Peta. And there was "Second Cousin Roko," the stubborn one who refused to leave and bought farm animals for a song from fleeing relatives. What did he know about all this?

The Phantom sat up suddenly. The farmer, Raimond, had been murdered because he had seen her. How about the children of the late Piotr? If it was known that they had also seen her, were they not also in danger? There could be no more rest this night. Devil was up watching him.

As he brushed the straw from his skintight costume—he had removed his outer clothes—he thought fleetingly of his sweetheart Diana Palmer in distant America. She was never far from his thoughts. He pictured her smile if she could see him sleeping on straw in this barn. He was unused to mattresses. He had been raised in a cave, with only a fur skin between himself and the cold rocky ground. When he and Devil visited her in her palatial home in Westchester County, a special room was put aside for man and wolf. A room bare of all furniture except two straw mats on the floor that served as their beds. Diana's mother never got used to that, or him!

Ah, Diana. He visualized her warm, beautiful eyes, her soft red lips, her cloud of chestnut hair. It had been a long time. It would be a long time, before he could see her again. He carefully folded his topcoat, trousers, scarf, hiding them with the hat under a pile of straw. He could travel easier and faster without these city clothes. He and Devil moved quietly out of the barn, so quietly that the only other occupants, field mice, did not even awaken.

He reached the sleeping little town and, avoiding the narrow streets, climbed up and moved over the rooftops. Devil remained in a secluded corner to wait for the return of his master. The Phantom paused on a tile roof higher than the rest and looked about. No light anywhere. No one on the street. Everyone in Koqania was either asleep or pretending to be. How to find the widow of Piotr and her children who had seen the witch? There were no handy telephone directories in this place. The police would know, but he couldn't go to them. The cabdriver? Where to find him? He considered the house he was standing on. Bigger than the rest with a small front lawn and picket fence. He recognized it. The cabby had pointed it out as the residence of the Lord Mayor of Koqania, a mighty-sounding title for this tiny place. His Honor might know.

He moved silently down the tile roof to the eaves, then lowered himself to a second-floor balcony. Perhaps His Honor addressed the people from this balcony. The French doors were locked. He listened. Heavy snoring came from inside. In his endless battle against criminals, the Phantom had learned all their tricks; he knew he had to be better than they were to defeat them. He knew how to open combination locks of safes and how to open locked windows and doors. He opened the French doors quickly and silently and moved into the room. There were heavy curtains on the windows and doors and the room was pitch-black—and filled with the tremendous snores of what must be a big man. The Phantom stood quietly for a moment as the noise reverberated through the room. Then he flashed his small light beam for an instant, illuminating the figure of a man with an enormous belly. The beam went on and off so quickly that the sleeper was undisturbed. This had to be the Lord Mayor. No one else could have such a huge belly, the Phantom thought with a grin. He moved to the bed, then lightly stroked the bald head. The man snorted and mumbled and rolled away. The light touch continued. The snoring suddenly stopped. He was awake.

"Your Honor, do not be afraid," said the voice in the dark.

It is a scary thing to be awakened in a dark room by a strange voice. The Phantom knew that a man with a weak heart might have an attack. His voice was soft and reassuring.

"Relax. You are safe. Do not be afraid."

After a moment, the Lord Mayor replied in a choked voice, "Who are you?"

He reached for a bedside lamp. This was one of the few houses in Koqania with electricity, supplied by its own generator. But the Phantom stopped the hand. The Lord Mayor withdrew his as though he had touched a snake.

"No light," said the Phantom. "I have a question. Then you can sleep."

"What?" The Lord Mayor replied hoarsely.

"A man named Piotr was killed. Where are his widow and children?"

The man in bed gasped and almost choked.

"Are you, are you a—?" he began frantically, trying to sit up. He trembled violently as the Phantom's hand held him firmly.

"No, I am not a vampire," said the Phantom sharply. "I have come to destroy them."

The Lord Mayor digested the statement slowly.

"Destroy the vampires? Is this a trick?"

"No trick. Have you seen them?"

"No."

"Have you seen the witch?"

A sharp intake of breath.

"Oh, no, n-n-not her."

"Where is she?"

"With them."

"Where are they?"

"Find them and you'll find her."

"Where is the widow of Piotr and her children?"

"Hidden away."

"Why?"

"Afraid."

"Hidden where?"

The Lord Mayor was silent, his eyes searching the blackness, trying to make out his visitor. The hand squeezed his arm. He would find black-and-blue marks on it the next day. ("Sometimes the Phantom forgets how strong he is"—an old jungle saying.)

"Tell me."

"In the sanctuary of the church."

The Lord Mayor lay quietly, waiting for the next question. The pressure on his arm was gone. He tried to hear the breathing of the stranger. He heard nothing. Had the French doors opened and closed? He wasn't certain. It had happened so quickly, and the night outside was almost as dark as the room. He waited.

"Are you there? I mean, are you here?"

No answer.

He reached cautiously toward his bedside lamp. No restraining hand. He quickly snapped on the light and stared around the room. It was like waking from a nightmare. Had it happened? Was he dreaming? He took a pistol from the bedside table drawer, then got up and turned on a few more lamps. No one else was in the room. He examined the closed French doors. They were unlocked. He often forgot to lock them. Had he locked them this night? He wasn't certain. He poured a small glass of brandy and downed it in a single gulp. Then poured another and took it to bed with him, leaving the lights on. The pistol remained on the blankets, on top of the big mound made by his stomach. Had there really been a visitor in the dark? The next morning, he would find a mark on the bedside table like a skull, or a death's head.

The sanctuary of the church. Of course. One place vampires could not go. He moved back over the rooftops toward the high church steeple. There was a high stone wall surrounding the church grounds, a small graveyard, the old stone church and a small attached building that must be the rectory. He dropped lightly to the ground and moved through the graveyard. There was a shuffling sound. He froze behind a gravestone and stared into the darkness. The night was dark and the overhanging trees made it darker. Even with his practiced night vision, he could see no movement. He glanced back at the wall. The area above it was open and lighter. He might have been seen coming over. A moment later, as he moved forward slowly, he realized he had been seen. There was a soft swishing sound. The speed of his jungle-trained reactions probably saved his life. In that split second, he ducked to one side as an iron bar struck a glancing blow on the side of his head. Had it hit him directly, it could have killed him. The blow was hard enough to knock him out for a moment. He fell to the ground. There was a quick indistinct whisper above him. Then the sound of feet running on the pebble path. He remained motionless. The iron bar might be poised over his head. He strained his ears. No sound of breathing nearby. He concentrated on his skull, "feeling" it without touching it. A slight drop of blood. A fracture? By this time, his head was clearing. Then in one quick move, he was on his knees with a gun in his hand. He was alone.

He remained motionless for another moment . . . distant sounds of running feet on cobblestones. Who had hit him? He'd seen nothing. But there was a trace, a scent of alcohol, a mixture of beer and brandy. It might be anyone in the town. He got to his feet and moved unsteadily to the rectory wall. His head ached, but as he pressed the spot with his fingers he knew that the blow had done no harm. The whole episode had lasted no more than a minute. What was going on in this sanctuary of the church? Was he too late? Perhaps. The door was ajar.

He flashed on the thin beam of his flashlight. A man was lying on the floor wearing a burlap robe tied at the waist with a rope. A monk or a priest? He lay very still. A victim of that same iron bar? The man was breathing slowly. Still alive. There was a sobbing sound from further down the corridor. He moved to it. Beyond a doorway, a single candle burned on a wooden table. Huddled in a corner of the room was a woman whose face seemed frozen in horror. As her terrified eyes focused on him, her body jerked. She screamed. He reached her in one stride, and put his big hand on her mouth.

"Shh, I am your friend," he whispered. And repeated that until the violent spasms of her body ended. Whatever she had been through, he knew that the sight of him in his mask and skintight costume was not reassuring.

"Are you Piotr's widow?"

That name seemed to bring her back to reality. She looked at him tensely.

"Are you one of them?"

"I am not a vampire," he said. "I have come to destroy them." She looked at him blankly for a moment. It all seemed more than she could handle. She shook with another spasm, and she seized his hand so tightly that her fingernails dug into his skin.

"They took my children. We thought we were safe here.

That's what everybody said. We were safe here—safe here—safe here." She kept repeating it as though repetition would make it so.

"Why did they want your children?"

Her voice sank to a whisper as her eyes darted about the room. "Because they saw her. They saw the old witch."

"Where?"

"Oh, God, what have they done to my children?"

"Where did they see the old witch?"

"Get my children. Get them. *Get them!*"

"When did they take your children?"

"Get them. Get them. Get them."

He could learn nothing more from her. She was in shock. Whatever had happened was still too fresh.

"I will find them. Listen to me: that priest out there tried to stop them. He is hurt and needs help. Help him j right away." This appeal reached her and brought some sanity back into her eyes. She nodded and began to weep and rock back and forth.

"Right away," he said. "Now."

He rushed out of the room, paused to make sure the man was still breathing, then rushed on. Outside, he vaulted onto the low rectory roof and ran to the adjoining church roof. He reached the stone steeple and began to climb. Up there the darkness was less oppressive. The glow of eternal starlight faintly lit the scene. He could see the outlines of the roofs and gables of the town. As he reached the bell tower, he breathed a brief nonsectarian prayer for a break in the heavy cloud cover overhead. There was some light, but not enough. Perhaps his proximity on that church steeple helped. There was a brief break in the clouds, and the moonlight shone through. The ancient town was briefly lighted as if by a magic lantern. Then the opening closed and the darkness returned. But that moment had been enough.

Barely a block from the church wall, he saw several dark figures carrying unwieldy bundles that seemed to jerk and writhe in their arms. He moved down quickly, dropping the last twenty feet to land in a crouch on the lawn. He raced over the grass along the wall, and so light were his steps that he seemed to float. Then he stopped. On the other side of the wall there were heavy footsteps on the cobblestones, grunts and gasps from men carrying burdens, and small muffled sounds that were high little voices crying through gags. He vaulted onto the seven-foot wall, hesitated momentarily, then dropped on the dark figures below. Two men and their bundles collapsed under him with exclamations of pain and surprise. A third dark figure raised a heavy pipe. Busy with the squirming mass under him, the Phantom lashed out with one foot, catching the pipe wielder in the stomach. The man fell back; the pipe fell to the stones and with a clang. That was the man he wanted, the one with the iron pipe, but he scrambled away while the Phantom grappled with the two men under him. This all happened in a few seconds. The Phantom, conscious of the writhing bundles and trying to protect them, rolled to one side, dragging the cursing, fighting men with him. One of his hands reached a throat. He grasped it firmly and banged the head against the cobblestones. The owner of that head was instantly quiet. ("The Phantom is rough with roughnecks"—an old jungle saying.)

With his other hand, the Phantom was pushing the writhing bundles out of the way to avoid injuring them. During this quick action, the second man jumped to his feet and ran as though pursued by devils. He got away. The violent action was over almost as quickly as it had begun. The bundles whimpered softly. He stood up and quickly surveyed the surrounding area. The two men were out of sight, their feet clattering along in the distance. No time to get them now. He raised the bundles to a sitting position, then spoke to them quietly.

"I am your friend. Your mother sent me to bring you back to her," he said.

The whimpering stopped. That magic word "mother" had done it. He untied the black sacks and peeled them off, revealing the two children, a boy and a girl, hands and legs tied, mouths gagged. But their eyes were open wide.

"Shh, the bad men are near. We must be very quiet," he said softly. They nodded. The girl was trembling. The older boy took her hand.

"Are you our friend?" he asked.

"I am your friend. Come. Your mother is waiting for you." He slung the unconscious man over his shoulder, then led the two along the wall to a gate. But the gate was locked. He put the man down, and boosted each child to the top of the high wall. They waited while he slung the man on top of the wall, then vaulted up. He lowered the children to the ground inside, then dropped down with the man over his shoulder.

There was candlelight in the rectory hall. The children's mother was sitting on the stone boor holding a candle near the fallen priest. She looked up with startled eyes. Then her face relaxed as the children rushed to her. There were hugs and kisses and cries of relief. The Phantom waited patiently. These people had had a terrible experience. When they had calmed down, the woman looked at the masked man, then at the priest.

"I tried to lift him to a cot, but he's too heavy for me."

The Phantom nodded, and carried the man to a cot in a sparsely furnished cell-like room.

"All you can do for him now is let him sleep. Get a doctor in the morning—is there a doctor?"

She nodded. The Phantom picked up the man he had brought into the rectory and they moved into a small chapel where several candles were burning in little red glasses, casting an eerie light.

Mother and children looked anxiously at the dark figure on the floor. The man wore a black suit and had lost his hat. He wore a black handkerchief for a mask. The Phantom pulled it off.

"Do you know him?"

They looked at him fearfully, then shook their heads. "Must be a stranger from out of town."

He had a small sandy mustache, sandy hair, and a two-days' growth of beard. He seemed familiar. The Phantom realized he had been among those at the tavern earlier in the evening, an inconspicuous fellow sitting in the back with a mug of beer.

"Now tell me what happened here."

Among the three of them, they told the story. Three masked men (they looked fearfully at the Phantom's mask) had broken in, assaulted the priest, and dragged the children out without saying a word.

"Without a word?"

"Nothing."

"Maybe some of them were afraid you'd recognize their voices."

"Recognize vampire voices?"

"What makes you think they were vampires?"

"What else?"

"Does this one look like a vampire?"

He looked quite ordinary.

"If they weren't vampires, why did they come?" said the mother. She was a strong peasant woman and was regaining her strength and composure rapidly.

"I don't know. We'll find out."

"Who are you?" asked the boy.

"Your friend," said the Phantom. "Now tell me quickly, where did you see the witch?"

The children looked fearfully at their mother. She nodded. "Tell him."

"Up in the old ruins."

"Tell me what you saw."

They appeared afraid to talk about it. It had been a scary experience. Patiently, he drew it out of them. They had been climbing in the ruins, against their mother's orders, as she reminded them sternly. They heard strange sounds.

"Like what?"

"Like somebody who was hurt."

"Moaning and groaning?"

"Yes, like that," said the boy eagerly. "And we peeked through an old window that had bars on it, and we saw her."

"What did you see?"

Both children started to talk at once. He stopped them to get a clear picture.

"It was an old lady, very old, lots of wrinkles and long white hair down to here." The girl pointed to her waist. "And she was tied to a post."

"Tied to a post?"

"With chains, iron chains. And she moaned and she groaned."

The Phantom's mind reeled for a moment. What had Old Mozz said, so far away in the Deep Woods? "He chained her securely to a pillar of stone, and she shrieked and she wailed."

"Was she chained to a wooden post?" he asked softly. "No, to a stone post," said the boy.

"Are you sure you saw this?"

"Oh, yes. We saw it, didn't we," said the boy.

The girl nodded anxiously.

"They saw what everyone has always known, that the old witch of Hunda is chained there through eternity for she was evil and that is her punishment," said the mother, as though repeating an old ritual.

Hunda? The chronicles, three hundred years ago, called her 'Hanta.'

"How many people did you tell about this?"

The children thought for a moment.

"We told mama and daddy," their faces twitched with pain at the thought of their late father. "We told Uncle Roko."

"Uncle Roko?"

"My brother," said the mother.

Naturally, almost everyone in this tiny place was related. That made Roko the late Piotr's brother-in-law.

"Did he offer to buy your land and animals?"

"He offered to help. He is my brother," she said, looking confused at this turn in the talk.

He looked through the chapel window. There was a light gray line in the sky.

"It is almost dawn. I must go. Does your brother live by the crossroads beyond the town in the big brown house?"

"Yes. Off Cemetery Road."

"When daylight comes, you have nothing to fear. The three

of you go together to get a doctor for the priest."

"Then we will tell the police."

"No, not yet." He couldn't have them blundering so close to his trail now.

"Thank you for helping us," said the mother.

"Mister, if you hadn't found us, what would they do to us?" asked the little boy.

"Nothing much. Make you stand in the corner."

He smiled and his voice was light as he said that. Who knows what horrible fate had been intended for them?

They smiled at their mother. She hugged and kissed them. When they looked up, the stranger was gone.

"Wasn't he nice?" said the girl.

"Why did he wear a mask like those bad men?"

The mother's eyes suddenly widened.

"He said he had to leave because it was almost daylight."

"Mama, isn't that what they have to do?"

The children stared at their mother. Was that a vampire, too? Could there be a good vampire? They huddled together. This world of Koqania had become a terrifying place.

CHAPTER 11

A s he raced to the edge of town with Devil, who had been waiting patiently all the while, dawn was breaking in the east. In distant houses, people were moving out of doors to start their morning chores. As he reached his deserted barn, he could see a few carts coming down the road, some piled high with household articles. More families fleeing? Inside the bam, he lowered his hood, and using rainwater from an old trough, he bathed his head. There was a small break in the skin. The bleeding had stopped. A lucky escape from more serious injury. He opened the small emergency kit that accompanied him everywhere, applied antiseptic ointment and a small patch, then replaced the hood.

It had been quite a night. First, the snoring Lord Mayor, then the men in black, then the widow and children. Why had her husband Piotr been killed? At least now he knew that the so-called vampires, whoever they were, were not imaginary. The bump on his head was proof of that. Why had they kidnapped the children? To kill them? In that case, why carry them off? To use them in some ghoulish ceremony? Was it all because they had seen the witch? So it seemed. Who knew that they had seen the witch? Their late father, mother, and her brother Roko, the stubborn one who wouldn't move, who bought terrorized neighbors' farm animals at bargain prices and perhaps their land as well. The big brown house off Cemetery Road, where Roko lived, was the next stop.

He stretched out on the straw with Devil next to him, and slept for an hour. Like the jungle animals they knew so well, both man and wolf slept with "one eye open," able to instantly awake from deep sleep on a moment's notice when danger threatened. Like the jungle animals— except the lordly lion who slept twelve or fourteen hours every day because he feared nothing—the Phantom was used to quick cat-naps, taken at odd times. He awoke after an hour, refreshed and rested.

He watched the country road, Old County Road, from the bam door. Normally, it would be busy with traffic from the farms to town. Now, only an occasional wagon rumbled by, always heavily loaded, with women and children perched on top, a man leading the horse. More rarely, a car bounced by on the bumpy dirt road, usually an ancient jalopy. One car was not ancient. It was a long shiny closed car and it raced over the road. He could only see vague figures inside.

It was time to eat. His last meal had been a quick sandwich at a train station more than twenty-four hours earlier. Devil was hungry, too. The Phantom petted his big gray companion, and said a single word, "Eat." Devil dashed out of the barn. The Phantom carried enough firepower to drop a big deer or a bear. But he would do no hunting now. He waited. Ten minutes later, Devil trotted in, carrying a freshly killed rabbit in his jaws. He dropped his catch at the Phantom's feet, received a rewarding pat, then turned and ran out again. While he was gone, the Phantom quickly skinned and dressed the animal, sharpened a skewer out of wood in the barn, then built a small fire. He placed the animal on the skewer, the skewer on two uprights on either side of the fire, and slowly roasted the meat. Devil returned with another catch. Rabbits were plentiful here, it seemed. Probably more so now that the humans were leaving. Devil lay on the floor with the kill between his paws and watched his master. The wolf was hungry, but he waited. When the meat was properly roasted, the Phantom stamped out the fire.

He sat next to Devil and held the roast poised in the air, ready to eat. The wolf watched him sharply, as he slowly brought the roast near his lips. Devil's jaws slowly approached the kill between his paws. The man held the roast tantalizingly close to his own mouth. The hungry wolf's jaws were a half inch from his own meal, but he waited. Then the Phantom suddenly bit into the roast, and Devil tore into his meal. It was a game both enjoyed and often played. The Phantom added a little salt to his meal, another item he always carried in his kit. There was an old well a short distance from the bam. Making certain he wasn't being observed, he drew pure cold water from it with the old wooden bucket for Devil and himself.

The meal finished, they swept their eating place with straw, leaving no trace of their activity. Then the Phantom donned his outer city clothes. It was easier to travel in daylight with the civilian outfit covering his skintight costume. He avoided the road, moving through the woods that banked the fields. The police—that odd pair—would be looking for him, especially the fire-eater, Sergeant Malo. The sight of a stranger with a "dog" would be reported. He moved carefully among the trees toward the brown house on the hill off Cemetery Road.

In response to his knock, a pair of suspicious eyes peered through an opening in the window shutters. The eyes looked at the big man and the gray animal. He knocked again. A rough voice came through the locked door.

"What do you want?"

"I want to talk to you, Roko."

The door opened a few inches. The man inside had a rifle. He was stocky, with a bald head, strong jaw, and thick neck. He was wearing brown denim trousers.

"I told you people to let me alone. I'm not interested," he said angrily.

"What people?"

"Aren't you with the ones that came here yesterday and the day before that?"

"No."

"You another buyer?"

"No."

"Then what in damnation do you want?"

"Who is it, Jebbon?" said a woman's voice inside.

"I don't know."

"Tell him to go away," continued the voice, more shrilly now.

"What do you want?"

"To talk to you."

"About what?"

The Phantom watched the rifle. The barrel was pointed at his waist.

"Let's talk inside, Roko."

"You got a name?"

"Walker."

"We can talk like this. Talk."

"I want to know about the vampires and the witch of Hunda."

The rifle jerked up as the man jolted with surprise. The Phantom's hand darted to the rifle barrel, turning it aside as it blasted into the doorframe. Inside, the woman screamed. The Phantom twisted the rifle out of Roko's hands and at the same moment kicked open the door, knocking Roko back so he fell to his knees. The Phantom moved in with Devil and the rifle, and slammed the door behind him. A middle-aged woman peeling potatoes at a table stared at him in terror.

"I came to talk to you, not to hurt you. Relax," he said quietly.

"I didn't mean to fire. The gun just went off," said Roko, backing away on his knees, his face still showing terror.

"I might believe that. That depends. Get up, Roko."

Roko climbed slowly to his feet. He was a heavy man, and had hurt his knees falling.

"Depends on what?"

"What else you tell me. Sit down."

Roko sat at the table next to his wife. She had dropped her paring knife into the wooden bowl of potatoes. She clutched her husband's hand in terror. The couple stared at the big stranger.

"First, tell me what you know about the vampires."

"Are you . . . one of them?" said Roko.

"You know better than that."

"How would we know?" said the wife shrilly.

"Shh," said her husband. "She is right. We've never seen them. We've heard them."

"When?"

"Every night for the last few weeks. Moaning and scratching outside the house."

"Moaning and scratching," repeated the wife, shaking as though describing a nightmare.

"What did you do?"

"Nothing. I wanted to go outside and shoot them. She wouldn't let me," said Roko.

"You can't shoot them. Bullets don't bother them. Chief Peta tried," said Mrs. Roko.

"The police chief? How do you know?"

"He told us. He's my cousin," said the woman, stressing the relationship proudly.

More of these family connections. Was everyone in Koqania related?

"When your neighbors moved out, you bought their farm

animals at very low prices."

"I gave all I could. They had to have some money. No one else would buy. They're all afraid," he added scornfully.

"Aren't you afraid?"

"Yes, every night."

"Every night," echoed the woman.

"I worked all my life to make this a good farm. Nobody's driving me off—not even vampires. They'll have to carry me off dead!" he shouted, his heavy face reddening.

"He keeps saying that," said the wife angrily. "But I'm not putting up with this much longer. The next time those men come, we're selling."

"We are not. I'll never sell to those thieves."

"What men?"

"I don't know who they are. They gave me their card, but I can't read," he added apologetically.

"Have you bought land from the people who left their farms?"

"I don't have that kind of money." He looked at his wife and shrugged.

"He wanted to," she shouted. "Wanted our life savings. All my milk and egg money. 'No! I said. 'No!' "

"It was such a temptation. The farm next door—so cheap. Going for a song and nobody else wanted it. Better than mine. I watched it all my life. Then with Piotr dead—"

"Your brother-in-law."

Roko looked at him sharply.

"How did you know that?"

"What about the witch?"

Husband and wife stared at him. This word always seemed to stun these people.

"We never saw her," Roko stammered. "But Elise and Tondo did. They're Piotr's children."

"How do you know that?"

"They told us right here at this table," said the wife. "They saw her down there. She was old, and chained to a stone pillar, and she moaned and groaned," continued the wife, terrified by the image she was describing.

"When did you first hear about the witch?"

"When? All our lives. She's always been there."

"Did anyone see her when you were children?"

They tried to remember. They looked at each other.

"Some said they did."

"Anybody you knew?"

"It's hard to remember," said Roko.

"Who did you tell that Piotr's children saw the witch?" The couple looked at each other, puzzled. They shook their heads.

"Nobody."

"Now about those people who are trying to buy this place. Have they bought other farms?"

"Yes, several. All for nothing. The cheap—!" he said with a string of Koqania oaths.

"Jebbon!" said his wife reprovingly.

"You said they gave you a card. A business card?"

"I guess that's what it was."

"Have you got it?"

Roko glanced at his rifle in the stranger's hands. "Can I get up?"

"Yes."

He went to an old bureau and began going through the drawers.

"I put it away someplace, didn't I, Enna?"

"I don't know. I don't look at your things."

There was a sound of a motor outside, an automobile. Roko looked through the shutters.

"It's them!" he cried. "I told them not to come back." He turned to the Phantom.

"You want to talk to them?"

"Not yet. You talk to them. I don't want to be seen— understand?" Roko nodded, understanding nothing. He pointed to a closet with a drapery for a door. The Phantom stepped behind it.

Roko opened the door. Since the Phantom still had his rifle, he was unarmed.

"We've come back to talk about your land, Mr. Roko," said one man. The Phantom peered through the wall. This was not difficult since the old siding was warped and there were many cracks. He could see the speaker, a stout, well-dressed man in dark city clothes. He had a foreign guttural accent.

"I told you yesterday, and the day before, it is not for sale," said Roko. He spoke respectfully, evidently impressed by these city men in their expensive clothes.

"Please understand that we are buying most of the land in this valley to farm on a big scale. The small farms are no longer economical. They are doomed. We intend to bring modern farming methods here." He spoke convincingly, like a bond salesman. The other man remained quiet. He was bigger, heavier, also well dressed.

"You told me all that before," said Roko.

"Only two or three farms in this area remain unsold. Yours is one of them. We will raise our offer to four thousand levana."

Roko snorted. "I have three hundred hectares. My land is worth ten times what you offer."

"The value of land depends on the availability of a buyer," said the spokesman. "Who else would buy your land today?"

"I told you. I'm not selling," said Roko, his voice louder now. "That's my final word!"

"That is unfortunate, Mr. Roko," said the man almost sadly. "Because we must obtain this farm to complete our plans. Here is our last and final offer, five thousand levana."

The Phantom peered through the cracks, wondering if there were other men as well. The car was out on the road, the motor idling. It was the big, expensive car he had seen earlier in the day. More men were inside, he saw, but too far away to be seen clearly.

"No to five thousand. No to twenty thousand. This land was my father's and my grandfather's before him. I was born here. I will die here," said Roko angrily.

"That is touching, Mr. Roko. But you are letting sentiment outweigh your good sense. I told you, we must have this land—at a fair price, of course."

"No, this is our home," said Roko, shouting angrily.

"Home? This old dump?" said the man, nasty now.

"Is it fair to keep your wife in this pigpen when she could have a decent stone house in town with a real tile roof?" he added scornfully. Like all Koqania farms, Roko's house had a thatched roof of straw. This was too much for Roko. He had the best house in the district.

"Get out. Get off my land!" he shouted.

The spokesman nodded to his silent companion. "Hans," he said. The big man grabbed Roko by the collar and banged his head against the doorframe. The wife screamed. Roko was big and heavy, but no match for this one called Hans.

"Hans has orders to make you accept our offer, if he has to break every bloody bone in your body," said the spokesman, no longer the polite bond salesman.

The Phantom bounded out of the closet, leaving the rifle behind. As he reached the door, Hans punched Roko hard in the stomach. Roko doubled up with pain and fell to his knees. Hans and the spokesman looked up in surprise as the big stranger filled the doorway. Hans, with steely eyes and a battle-scarred jaw, asked no questions but aimed a punch that never landed. Instead, an iron fist smashed against his jaw. Hans flipped over backward, off the veranda onto the ground. The spokesman was reaching inside his coat (for a gun?) when the Phantom grabbed him, lifted him into the air, and hurled him on top of Hans. The two men scrambled around in the dirt, then a horn sounded from the automobile. The two jumped to their feet and, without a backward glance, ran to the car. It began to move before they reached it. The doors were open and they leaped in. The car picked up speed and vanished over the hill.

Roko was sitting on the floor staring at his rescuer, Mr. Walker.

"You are something," he gasped, holding his stomach. He had taken a hard blow. The Phantom helped him to his feet and walked him to the table where he sat down heavily. His wife was almost hysterical.

"That settles it," she cried. "I won't stay any longer in this crazy place. Sell it! Sell it to anybody! I want to get out."

"You've held out this long. Try a little longer," said the Phantom.

"Hold out for what? Until we go crazy?" she cried.

"She's been at me to sell ever since the troubles started. I'm the one who's held out. Maybe she's right—a man can go just so long."

"True. You're a brave pair to hold out this long. It must have been a nightmare for you," said the Phantom.

"That it has been—a nightmare," said the woman.

"I'm here to help you and all your neighbors."

"Who are you, Mr. Walker? Some kind of policeman?" asked Roko.

"No," said the Phantom. "I must ask one more question about the witch of Hunda."

The couple tensed at the word. Their eyes darted from side to side.

"Shh, you said that name before," said Roko softly, glancing around the room as though the walls might have ears.

"Why are you afraid to talk about her?"

"She hears everything that goes on. She knows," said the wife.

"How do you know that?"

"It has always been like that."

"Since you were children?"

"Since our grandfathers and their grandfathers were children."

"The children of Piotr said they saw her. Where?"

"On the hill, in the ruins," said Roko.

"Shh," said his wife sharply. "Why are you putting your

nose in our business?"

"Enna, is that the way to talk to him after he saved me? That damn thug might have killed me," said Roko.

"Mind your tongue, Jebbon Roko. This is not a tavern," snapped the woman. "Saved you? Saved you from selling this accursed place. Nobody else will buy it. Who are you, mister?"

An automobile motor sounded outside as a car approached the house.

"They've come back," said Roko, jumping up.

"Where's my rifle?"

"Jebbon, if they want to buy, sell!" shouted the woman.

The Phantom peered through the shutters. It was not the big shiny car. It was a small pickup truck. Sergeant Malo was at the wheel.

"It's Sergeant Malo. He may be looking for me," said the Phantom. "You are not to tell him I am here. Is that clear?" He looked at them briefly through his dark glasses, then stepped back into the closet. Roko opened the door in answer to the knock.

"Malo?" he said curtly, his tone barely concealing a dislike for the policeman.

"Sergeant Malo," was the equally curt reply. "Have you seen a stranger around here?"

"Stranger?"

"A big man."

"Yes."

Inside the closet, the Phantom crouched, ready to leap out.

"Go on. Where did you see him?" asked Malo.

"Him? More than one. A big man. A short fat one. They came in a long black automobile. They've been here before trying to buy this land."

"Not them," said Malo with some irritation. "This man is alone. He has a dog, a big gray dog."

"Didn't see a big gray dog," said Roko, mimicking Malo's tones. He spoke the truth. Devil had remained outside hidden in the high grass.

"Did you see him?" said Sergeant Malo to Enna, the wife. She looked at her husband. Her fists were clenched under the table. Inside the closet, the Phantom waited tensely. If she glanced in his direction, it would be enough to send Malo, or a bullet, through the drapery.

"Speak up, woman," said Sergeant Malo impatiently.

Whatever she had been about to say died on her lips as she glared at the swarthy policeman.

"I have a name," she snapped.

"You don't call my wife 'woman' in my home or any place else. Sergeant Malo," said Roko angrily.

Through a tiny opening in the drapery, the Phantom had a partial view of Malo. His face turned red and his hand brought his gun halfway out of the holster.

"People who obstruct justice end up behind bars or worse!" he shouted, working up a violent rage as he had done in the chiefs office. The Phantom knew this man was capable of shooting Roko in cold blood. He moved his own hand silently toward one of his concealed guns. But the violence died as quickly as it had begun.

"I've done no 'obstructing.' I have a witness," said Roko coolly, glancing at his wife, the cousin of Chief Ivor Peta, a fact that Malo knew well.

"Damn you," he said, and turning smartly on his heels in military fashion, stamped out of the house to his car, and sped away.

The couple laughed, the first time they'd been able to do so in a long time. The Phantom came out of the closet. They'd almost forgotten him.

"Thank you," he said.

"Why is he after you?" asked Roko.

"He doesn't like me."

"Join the crowd. He doesn't like anybody."

"And nobody likes him. He's mean and nasty," said Enna. "I don't know why cousin Ivor keeps him on."

"Because he does all the work and keeps your precious cousin supplied with schnapps," said Roko.

The Phantom was looking out the window. Sergeant Malo's truck was moving along the road that led to the ruins. He watched for a few minutes. The vehicle turned, came back, then turned again. He appeared to be patrolling the road.

"Do you mind if I stay here until he goes?" '

"You're welcome to," said Roko.

"I've got my housework to do," his wife said peevishly.

"I'll stay out back, in your barn, until dark."

"It's not very clean," said Roko apologetically.

"It's clean enough," snapped the woman.

The Phantom smiled at her, and she smiled in spite of her bad humor. There was something attractive about this big quiet man. His voice for one thing. Deep and strong.

"Excuse me. I'm not myself. I'm so nervous these days," she said.

"You have every right to be. You are a brave woman," he

said. "Perhaps we will meet again." And he slipped, out the back door. They watched him move swiftly into the bam. There was a soft whistle. A big gray shape bounded out of the grass and ran into the bam.

"I wonder who he is," said the woman.

"Mr. Walker, whoever that is," said Roko.

They busied themselves with their chores, fixed another meal, discussed the exciting events of the day, occasionally looked out at the bam but saw no movement (perhaps he was gone), lit kerosene lamps, and were preparing for bed when they heard the moaning and scratching outside the house.

CHAPTER 12

"Come out. We want you," moaned the voices— scratching on the side of the house—"We want you. Come out." Husband and wife clutched each other. It was night outside, no moon, and the vampires had returned.

"Jebbon, that Mr. Walker who was here. Maybe he's really one of them?" gasped Enna.

"Can't believe that, I just can't. He helped us."

"Helped us? Saved us for himself," cried the wife, shaking with terror now and grasping her husband tightly. He pulled her arms away, looked about the room wildly, then went to the closet and got his rifle.

"No, Jebbon . . . you can't go out there. Bullets won't stop them."

"Come out. Come out. We want you." Moans and shrill laughter now, and scratching.

Roko pulled open a window, pushed aside the shutter, and fired wildly into the darkness. There was wild laughter from another side of the house . . . then something struck Roko in the face. He staggered away from the window, momentarily blinded by a lump of cow manure.

There was a sudden blaze of firelight outside.

"Come out or we'll burn your house down," called the

voices. "Come out. Come out."

Wiping his face on his sleeve, Jebbon edged along the wall near the window. Enna, speechless with terror, stood pressed against a back wall. As Roko peered out, trying to identify the firelight, a large rock crashed through a windowpane. Enna screamed. Outside, fire glowed from behind a boulder. As Roko peered breathlessly from the corner of the window, he could see two black figures—in capes and big hats—he had a dim impression of white, white faces . . . exactly as many had described them—the vampires! In fear and anger, he raised his rifle again. Fire sailed through the air like a rocket. It was a flaming torch, thrown from behind the boulder by a dark figure. It landed on the thatched roof. Jebbon and Enna stared in terror at the ceiling. A few wisps of smoke came through. In minutes, the roof would turn into a flaming inferno over their heads.

"Come out. Come out, or we'll burn your house down," called the mocking voices. And another burning torch sailed through the dark night, landing on the roof.

"The house is on fire," screamed Enna.

Roko grabbed her hand.

"We can't stay here. Let's go!"

"No," she screamed again. "That's what they want. They're waiting for us—the vampires!"

"We can't wait to bum to death!" shouted Roko. He pulled her with one hand toward the door, his rifle in the other hand. But as they reached the door and Roko flung it open, a strange figure flashed out of the darkness. They saw it for only a second in the flickering torchlight—a lithe figure out of a dream. Then it jumped into the air and was lost from sight.

The Phantom had reached the roof in one powerful leap. He snapped up the torches that had just begun to ignite the straw and hurled them toward the boulder. He quickly stamped out the burning straw fragments, then was gone in the darkness. There was silence in the house and silence behind the boulder. What—who was that?

Roko slammed the door shut. Something had intervened to save them and their house. Whatever or whoever had done it—was he one of them or against them? His mind reeled. It was too much.

Behind the boulder, the dark figures muttered to each other. Then they turned and began to run away. A voice came out of the darkness near them.

"Wait, vampires. Don't you want me?"

A large figure was moving through the high grass toward them. The two muttered to each other again, then drew foot-long knives from their cloaks.

"Yes," said one in a heavy voice. "Whoever you are, we want you." And they rushed at the lone man, barely visible in the darkness. But when they reached the spot where he had been, he was not there. His voice came from another side.

"Over here," he said.

They turned and rushed toward the dim outline, knives held high, ready to stab and slash. When they reached their destination, only a few steps away, he was gone. They paused in confusion. Who was this man who could move like a will-o'-the-wisp? They made a quick, muttered decision—to get away fast. But they didn't make it. The dark figure suddenly loomed before them, and before they could lift their knives something like a rock or an iron bar struck twice within a split second, first one jaw beneath the wide black hat, then the other jaw. Both men dropped in their tracks.

Inside the house, Jebbon and Enna had heard the faint muttering and exclamations, but could make nothing out distinctly. Then silence. They stared at each other, wondering what would happen next. They didn't have long to wait. There was a dragging sound outside the door as though something heavy was being pulled along the grass onto the porch. Then a knock on the door. Roko raised his rifle, about to shoot through the door. Then he heard a familiar voice.

"Roko, it's me, Walker. Open up."

"No," cried Enna, afraid of everything now. But Roko went to the door and opened it. Standing in the doorway was the figure they had barely glimpsed in the flaming torchlight. A powerful figure, masked and hooded, in a skintight costume, a wide leather belt holding two guns in holsters, a gleaming insignia on the belt (a skull?). Dangling from each hand, held by the collar and lying limply on the ground, were the two dark figures who had thrown the torches.

"Mr. Walker?" said Roko, shaken by this unexpected sight.

"Yes, Jebbon and Enna, your friend. I changed my clothes." He whistled, and in a moment, a huge gray animal leaped through the doorway. Roko knew a wolf when he saw one. But he'd never seen one this big. He automatically raised his rifle.

"No, Roko," said Walker. "This is my friend. Sit, Devil."

The big animal with the long fangs and pale-blue eyes sat obediently, his head above the tabletop. Walker pulled the two men into the room and dropped them on the floor. They were obviously unconscious. The upper parts of their faces were covered with black kerchiefs. The lower halves were dead white, and two red-tipped fangs protruded from their mouths.

"The vampires. The walking dead!" cried Enna. 'Take them out of here." She ran to the end of the room, shuddering. Roko stood transfixed, afraid to look, too shocked to move. Vampires? In his house? And this weird figure, Mr. Walker?

"Mr. Walker" bent over the recumbent pair. He pulled off the hats and the kerchiefs. The upper half of each face about the nose and eyes had a normal complexion. The lower half, mouth and jaw, was covered with a white powder and something else—an odd, identical mark on each jaw. They were still a ghastly sight with their protruding crimson-tipped fangs. Blood? As Roko watched in horror and amazement, Mr. Walker reached down and pulled out the fangs. Obviously artificial, made of bone or plastic, they were the sort children use in their monster games.

"Here are your vampires. Recognize them?" said Mr. Walker.

"Enna," said Roko.

"No, I won't, I can't look," she said from the far end of the room.

"Don't be an old fool. Come here," said Roko impatiently. And from his tone, Enna knew somehow that the terror was gone. She joined him and stared at the unconscious men. One was powerful with a square jaw and scarred face—Hans. The other one was stout, the would-be land buyer of the afternoon.

"The vampires?" said Roko. "No, those are the men who tried to buy my farm."

"Those aren't the real vampires," said Enna. "They're imitating the vampires, trying to scare us."

"What makes you so sure these aren't the real vampires?" asked the Phantom.

"The real vampires are not fake. They are real," said Roko awkwardly. "I mean, we know that Ivor-Chief Peta—fired four shots into them and didn't hurt them at all."

"Five shots," said a belching voice at the door.

It was Chief Ivor Peta himself, swaying in the doorway, a gun in his right hand. He squinted his bloodshot eyes at the people standing in the room, at the men on the floor, at the big animal.

"Which one—hic!—is the vampire?" he demanded.

"Ivor," said Enna excitedly. "Thank God you're here. It's been terrible."

"I saw some light up here. Is that the vampire?" he said, his wavering gun pointing at the Phantom.

"No, Ivor," said Roko quickly. "That's Mr. Walker. He is our friend. He helped us."

Chief Peta stared at the strange figure that loomed like a giant in this small room.

"That's your friend?" he said. "Uh—what is he?"

"We met before in your office, Chief. I'm Walker."

Now it all came back.

"You're the one that made all that fuss? Say, you're the one I'm looking for," he said with a sudden delighted grin at this stroke of luck.

He waved his gun at the big silent figure. "Come along, you. Don't give me any more trouble. I've got a cell waiting for you."

"Chief, are you still drunk?" said the Phantom sternly. This unexpected question set the chief back.

"Me drunk? I'm sober as a judge."

"Really, Ivor, a man in your position," said Enna sharply. "I thank God my sainted Aunt Ruta didn't live to see you like this." Sainted Aunt Ruta would have been Chief Peta's mother, thought the Phantom.

"It's a lie. Sober as a judge," mumbled Peta, for the moment a boy facing a disapproving female cousin.

"We're wasting time," said the Phantom. "Come with me. We'll catch the real vampires."

He took the confused officer's arm and led him to the door.

"Roko, tie up those two phony vampires and guard them. The chief will book them later on charges of arson and attempted murder."

"I will?" said Chief Peta as the Phantom led him out the door to his little car.

"You will." The Chief started toward the driver's seat, but the Phantom pushed him into the other seat and took the wheel himself. He waved to the amazed couple in the doorway and drove off into the night.

"Who on earth is he?" said Enna once more.

"Mr. Walker. Whoever that is." Roko turned back into the house, got a coil of heavy rope and some light chain, and tied up the unconscious men with obvious pleasure. He bent lower over them.

"Enna, come look at this. Those marks on their jaws weren't there this afternoon. What do they look like to you?"

His wife looked where he pointed.

"Can't tell without my glasses."

"Both exactly the same—like what you see on bottles of poison stuff. You know. Death's heads," he said slowly.

Enna got her glasses, looked, and gasped.

"How'd they get there?"

"My guess is Mr. Walker. Know something else: my second guess is that's not his name."

CHAPTER 13

Chief Peta mumbled and belched as the car bounced and rumbled on the rough dirt road. Suddenly, he stiffened and turned pale. His hand reached for his gun. Out of the corner of his eye, he had seen a large, hairy shape directly behind him.

"Wha-wha-what?" he gasped.

"Relax, Chief. That's Devil. You saw him in your office."

"Uh, your dog?"

"He's a wolf."

"A wolf?" Koqania had wolves in the mountains. They killed sheep and goats and had been known to pull down steers.

"Don't be afraid. He's a friendly fellow, unless irritated."

Ivor Peta sat as far forward as possible. A vague thought whirled in his boozy brain.

"Some wolves can turn into vampires at night," he said frantically.

"No, Chief. You're thinking of werewolves."

"Oh."

The chief slumped back and started to doze. The road led into town. It was late at night. As usual, the streets were deserted. In the center square, opposite the Lord Mayor's mansion, was a large fountain that bubbled and cascaded forth water day and night. "Toss a levana in the fountain and you'll return to Koqania," travelers were told. No one did. No one wanted to come back. The Phantom stopped at the fountain, and after a quick look around pulled the half-dozing, protesting Chief Peta out of the car.

"Whazza matter?" mumbled the chief.

"You're drunk. No good to me at all this way."

"How do I know you're not a vampire—uhhh."

The Phantom picked him up and dropped him into the cold water. As Chief Peta gasped, he pushed his head under for a second, let him up to gulp air, then back under again. He repeated this a half-dozen times while the chief law officer of Koqania struggled, sputtered, gulped, and choked. When he began to swear, the Phantom pulled him out. The dripping police chief faced him. He was coughing up water and speechless with fury.

"You were too drunk. You're better now. Get back in the car."

He lead the wet policeman back to his seat. The man slumped gratefully in his place, then looked around anxiously.

"Did anyone see us?"

"Not a soul. Your dignity is intact."

And he drove on, through the dark empty streets, out of town. Chief Ivor Peta reached for cigarettes and matches. All were soaked.

"Damn," he said. "I'm sober now more or less. I need a cigarette."

"That can wait. We've got work to do."

"Who are you? What are you doing here?" said the chief, his eyes focusing properly for the first time all night as he stared at his strange driver—the hood, the mask, the skintight costume.

"Didn't you get a cable from Colonel Worobu of the Bangalla Jungle Patrol?"

"Uh, yes, the Jungle Patrol. Are you from there?"

"Yes."

"Did he send you?"

"In a way."

"That's a million miles from here. What business is our business to them?"

"Hmm, international ramifications," said the Phantom solemnly.

"International?" said Chief Peta, his eyes wide. "Uh, why do you wear that, er, odd outfit?"

"To scare the vampires."

The chief chuckled. "That's a good one." He sobered. "Look, this is no joke. They're real and they're—"

"I know."

"Hey, where are we going?"

The chief had looked out of the window. To his amazement, he saw the ruins of the old castle just ahead.

"We're going there."

"Now? Tonight? Alone?"

"Not alone. The three of us."

"Three?"

"You and I and Devil. He's worth twenty men."

The chief glanced back. Devil's long fangs gleamed in the pale light from the dashboard. The Phantom stopped the car, turned off the engine, and got out. Devil leaped over the front seat, out the same door, his long body brushing the chief who sat without moving. The Phantom crossed to the other side and opened the door. "Out," he said.

"Listen, Mr. Walker, or whoever you are, we can't go in there. That place is haunted."

"By vampires and a witch?"

"Yes. Vampires and the witch." He almost swallowed the last word. "But that's not all."

"There's more?"

"My grandfather saw him. Maybe he's one of them— one of the vampires."

"What did your grandfather see?"

"A kind of ghost. Hooded and masked like, like—" Chief Peta stared at his companion. "Say, you're—ah, foolish thought. That was fifty years ago."

He's talking about my grandfather, thought the Phantom. One of the generations of Phantoms who had visited this place since the days of the eighth Phantom.

"Let's go." He took the chiefs unwilling arm and they started through the high grass. Devil ranged ahead, going from side to side. "If there are any vampires hiding in the grass, Devil will flush them out."

As they neared the ruins, the chief balked.

"I don't like this. Not one bit."

"Would you rather we separate, you go around the back, I take the front?" said the Phantom. In answer, the chief clutched his arm.

"No, I stay with you."

"Okay, then in we go."

There were patches of clear sky now, and moonlight filtered through, throwing shadows among the ancient rocks. They crossed the moat on the rock pile and reached the dark staircase that led under the ruins. The chief stopped abruptly.

"We're not going down there?"

"Yes. Now quiet."

They reached the iron door. The Phantom turned his narrow light beam on in order to open the lock. But the lock was gone. The door was slightly open. The Phantom drew a gun from his holster. He had closed the lock the previous night, but he said nothing about this to the chief. That might have sent him into a panic. The door squeaked and groaned on its rusted hinges as he pulled it open. The two men and the wolf moved slowly along the damp stone corridor, the chief clutching the Phantom's arm in a tight grip. At each bend in the corridor, they paused. Then ahead, from around a bend, they saw flickering light. Chief Peta tensed, then shook with sudden fear. The Phantom patted his arm reassuringly and moved forward in a semi-crouch. A few steps ahead, Devil walked slowly, pale eyes gleaming, head lowered as though stalking.

They reached the turn in the corridor and peered around it. Ahead was the big rocky chamber with the many ancient devices of antique torture. A few torches in sockets were burning on the walls. The old metal of the torture instruments shone in the torchlight. Prominent among them was the shining hollow metal figure of the Iron Maiden. But most prominent, sitting on a low platform in the center of the chamber, was a coffin, the same coffin the Phantom had seen the previous day. But then it had been in a far corner, and he had left it closed. Now in the center of all these deadly devices, the coffin was open.

They stood without moving for a few seconds while the Phantom and Devil peered from spot to spot searching for movement. They saw nothing. At a touch from his master, the wolf moved silently about the chamber, searching through the shadowy and dark places: in corners, behind pillars and torture instruments. Then he returned to his master. The room was safe.

They started toward the coffin. Clutching the Phantom's arm, the chief held back, trembling now, on the verge of panic. This place was too much for his nerves. The Phantom pulled him along. They reached the coffin and looked in. It was not empty this time,

A figure was lying inside, a man wearing black formal attire, a white bow tie, a white dress shirt glittering with diamond studs. The face was dead-white. The eyes were open. A trickle of red blood was visible on his chin. Long fangs protruded from both sides of his mouth. And a large wooden stake protruded from his chest.

Chief Peta cracked at this sight. He screamed. He turned and ran as though pursued by all the demons of hell. His scream echoed among the rocky walls as he disappeared in the darkness, headed back toward the open air.

CHAPTER 14

The Phantom stared at the figure. As hardened as he was to the violent or unusual, this gruesome sight had given him a momentary shock. He reached out and touched the white cheek, then felt the chest under the fancy white shirt. Then he laughed, hearty laughter of relief and sheer amusement. The thing in the coffin was a wax dummy.

He turned and took a step back toward the direction the chief had fled in, then stopped. It was easier to work without the nervous officer, weakened as he was by alcohol and fear. By now, he would be headed for his car, and would soon be back in his office hitting the brandy bottle.

He studied the wax dummy. It was a clever, realistic job. Why would anyone go to all this trouble in this old cellar beneath the ruins? Not many outsiders would come here. At this moment in Koqania, it seemed more likely that nobody would dare to enter this place so widely known to be cursed and haunted. Then, why this theatrical prop, this gruesome scene, obviously intended to frighten? To frighten whom? Himself?

By now his presence, the presence of the stranger, would be known by whoever inhabited these ruins. The door had been left unlocked purposely. Torches lighted. He examined one. It couldn't have been burning for more than an hour or so. Was he being watched? Was the hunter being hunted?

His jungle-trained senses did not dismiss this possibility. Without doubt, there would be watchers in the night, eyes that had observed his going and coming, had seen Chief Peta flee. The chief, once safely back in town, could be counted on to tell what he had seen in the coffin and so enlarge the legend and increase the fear. But how about himself? What would they—the unknown watchers who had prepared this dummy and the torches—do about him? He would not wait to find out. He would find them first.

This chamber was as far as he had gone into the cellars. He saw dark corridors leading off at the far end. The old castle, its outbuildings and battlements, had covered many acres. That meant acres of cellars. He started toward the central dark corridor, and if there were eyes watching through chinks in the stone walls, he was unaware of them.

Something suddenly raced out of the darkness, and his gun moved toward it. The rapid patter of claws on stone. It was a huge rat as big as a cat. It sped out of the darkness across the torture chamber, headed for the open air. Quick as a flash, Devil was after it. The wolf had a long-standing feud with rats. Once in a deserted slaughterhouse, a pack of them had almost killed him. He killed the pack, but still bore the scars. Before the Phantom could stop him, he was out of sight. The master knew his animal's feelings about rats. Devil's chances of catching this big one were remote. The wolf would rejoin him when the chase was over.

Now the Phantom moved slowly and carefully through the dark corridor, the light from the torture chamber gradually diminishing. Soon he was in complete darkness. He flashed his thin beam only occasionally. A man walking in a dark place with a lighted flashlight was too easy a target. He moved slowly, testing each step. There could be ancient pits, wells, or trap doors down here. There could be subcellars, and cellars below that. He moved on, passing many empty chambers, all filled with the dust and neglected, stale air of many years.

He became aware of a strange sound, faint at first, then stronger as he went forward. It was a whirring or wheezing sound with an occasional rasping—a sound he couldn't place. As the sound became louder, he heard something else in the whirring and wheezing and rasping. A more human sound—wailing or a moaning? Could that be it? Moaning, wailing and what else? A faint shriek? Coming from somewhere ahead in these endless cellars.

He stood motionless in the darkness, shaken by these sounds. The words of Old Mozz, the teller of tales, came to him. He could almost hear the cracking voice . . . "there deep in the earth where none could see her, he chained her securely to a pillar of stone, for she was evil, this witch of Hanta. And so he left her. shrieking and moaning, and to this day she shrieks and moans."

As these words rang in his head, he heard another sound in the midst of the whirring, and wheezing, the rasping, the wailing and moaning. The most improbable sound of all. "Phantom. Phantom." It was a soft voice, a feminine voice, and it seemed to come from the walls and ceiling about him. He shook himself, flashed on his beam quickly, then turned it off. He had been able to see nothing but rough stone walls. "Phantom. Phantom." Suddenly, all the noises stopped. The wheezing, the whirring, the rasping, the moans, the wails, the shrieks—all gone. The cellar was as silent as a tomb.

What had caused those weird sounds? Wind whistling through the ruins? Old rafters creaking? Underground streams flowing? Animals. Birds? Insects? And that sound of his name? Imagination? That old tale of the witch of Hanta moaning and wailing. A story he refused to believe. None of his ancestors would chain a woman in a cellar and leave her to die, or moan through eternity, not even a witch. Yet that was the story of Old Mozz. And what had happened to the missing parchment page or pages in the eighth Phantom's chronicle of three hundred years ago? What else had Old Mozz told about that day? "This beauteous young creature turned into a shriveled old hag before his very eyes . . . but nothing can free her and nothing can return her to youth and beauty, nothing save the kiss of the Phantom."

Odd how those words kept ringing through his head as he stood in the damp underground corridor . . . he shook himself. I'm getting as superstitious as the rest of Koqania, he mused. Maybe it's catching, he thought, trying to see the humor in it. But he couldn't laugh. There was something strange going on down here, those strange noises, his name whispered in the dark. He stood for a moment, waiting to hear the soft sound of Devil returning. But there was no sign of his pet. Was he chasing the big rat through the fields? Or running into another rat pack? Devil could take care of himself and would find him. He moved on slowly in the direction from which all those sounds had come.

Now as he advanced slowly, gun in hand, he was aware of another sensation—a scent, an odor that reminded him of something. The image flashed into his mind. The dry sweet-moldy smell of dying flowers on a grave. He flashed on his beam. There was a faint mist near the ceiling. He turned off the light and moved on. The scent became stronger—dry, sweet, moldy—he began to feel dizzy. He walked on unsteadily, puzzled by what was happening to him. Perhaps it was best to turn back, find and breathe fresh night air. Then, ahead, there was a light in the darkness. And the sound started again: the wailing, the moaning, faint at first, stronger as he approached the light. The sweet scent was even stronger now. His dizziness was increasing. The wailing and moaning and the small shrieks became louder and louder. And out of the sound he heard that soft cry, "Phantom, Phantom."

Moving along the wall to keep on his feet, he reached the source of the light. It was an open doorway leading off the corridor. The sound was coming from there. The wailing, the moaning. Holding onto the doorframe, he peered in. There he saw her.

A shriveled old woman, dressed in faded rags, long white hair streaming down her shoulders. She was chained to a stone pillar. And as she slowly writhed, she wailed and moaned, and she called, "Phantom, Phantom."

CHAPTER 15

The moaning stopped. The chains rattled.

"At last, you have come to free me from my chains," she croaked in a weird singsong voice.

He leaned against the wall. The chamber seemed to revolve around him. What is the matter with me? I can hardly move, he thought.

"Come, free me, free me with a kiss," said the crackling voice. "Come."

The voice commanded. He crossed the room slowly as though fighting against a strong current in a stream.

"Further, further, another step. You chained me; you alone can unchain me."

It was like a nightmare, but it was real. Or was it? He had difficulty focusing his eyes. The chained figure swam before him. Wearily, using all his strength, he climbed the stone steps leading to the platform where she stood.

"One more step, one more step."

He was nearer now. Her eyes glittered. Her face was like old yellowed parchment, wrinkled beyond belief. Her wrinkled hands had long curving nails reaching toward his face.

"You took my youth and beauty. Make me young again."

He swayed before her.

"Free me, free me with a kiss."

Struggling to control himself, he stumbled toward her, aware now of her musty scent, the odor of ancient things. As he swayed, almost falling, she placed her face close to his and his lips brushed her rough cheek. At this moment, there was a tremendous clap of thunder that seemed to shake the chamber and resounded from wall to wall. In this same moment, the chains of the witch fell off and clanked onto the stone floor. She raised her arms.

"Free, free at last," she cried in her cracked voice as she moved away. He tried to stop her, but his movements were sluggish. He grasped the stone pillar for support. She paused in an archway and raised her thin hands with the long yellow fingernails.

"Free at last. You will not trap me again," she cried. And she limped out of sight. Dazed, he hung onto the pillar to keep from falling, then staggered after her.

"Wait, wait," he called. His own voice seemed to come from a distance. It was hard to move, like going through a deep swamp. He stumbled, caught himself, reached the wall, and using it for support he dragged himself to the archway where he had last seen her. It seemed to take ages before he got there. He peered in and a blaze of light startled him. He squinted, trying to make out what was ahead.

There were many candles set all over the large room in dozens of candelabra and wall sconces. He had the impression of gold furniture—a golden couch and flowers of all kinds in dozens of vases, giving off rich perfume. "It was the throne room, a huge ornate place, filled with hundreds of burning candles and thousands of flowers," Old Mozz had said.

And standing in the midst of the blazing candlelight and the banks of red, gold, and purple flowers was a shimmering golden object: a figure, a woman. He seemed to be seeing her through a mist, but as he staggered nearer he could see her more clearly. She was a beautiful young woman with long shining blonde, hair, large luminous eyes, smiling red lips, gleaming white teeth. She was clad in a shimmering robe—"a shimmering robe that seemed to reveal yet conceal the perfect ivory body beneath." Was she real, or like a mirage in the desert?

As he neared her, she moved gracefully behind a low table and she laughed, a low musical sound. He leaned on the table and, reaching across, touched her cheek lightly. It was smooth and soft, the skin of a young woman. She was real. Her eyes were bright, and her quick breathing and the rapid rise and fall of her bosom revealed excitement.

"Not too close," she said, drawing away. "Where have you come from, mysterious stranger in the night?"

The room seemed to be turning. She was turning with it. If both would only stop for a moment. If he could get his hands on her, find some reality in this weird dream. He reached again and almost fell. His strength was draining from him. This time she reached him, and her touch was light as a butterfly.

"Let me help you. Come this way, poor man. You are so tired . . . so tired."

Her voice was a gentle whisper. She took his arm and led him slowly across the room as he clutched at furniture to keep from falling. He brushed against candelabra and vases as he went, leaving a trail of burning candles and flowers on the floor behind him. This amused her and she laughed as each fell.

"Oh, you poor man, so tired and weak. You need rest," she whispered, and there was a promise of love and passion in her voice. He let her lead him, because her touch was gentle and her voice was soft with pleasure and promise. They reached an opening of some sort.

"One more step, precious man. One more step, mystery man of my dreams. One more step, lover."

He took one more step and suddenly her touch was gone as he pitched into the night air, falling headlong to where he landed with a loud splash. Her light laughter followed him. Then all blacked out as he sank into the dark waters of the moat. Never trust a witch.

Sometime later, he opened his eyes. A voice was ringing in his ears, a young fresh voice, saying, "One more step, lover." He looked up. A full moon was riding high overhead. He moved his head slightly, an effort since it throbbed and ached. A large figure was beside him. Pale eyes gleamed in the moonlight. A large tongue licked his hand. Devil.

He sat up slowly, moving his hands over his body, feeling for wounds or broken bones. None. He was soaking wet from head to foot. The moat . . . he saw that he was sitting a few feet from the edge of the dark water. He dimly remembered falling in. Had he climbed out? He felt bruises on his forearm. He examined them. Devil's teeth marks. He looked at the mud and grass at the edge of the moat, and understood. Devil had pulled him out. The rat chase had ended, and the wolf had found his master. Just in time, it seemed. He patted the big animal. Devil had saved his life.

He sat quietly for a moment. He was still dizzy; his head

ached, his mouth was dry, his stomach queasy. He remembered the mist, that sweet-sick smell of dying flowers, the walls and ceiling turning. Had some kind of natural effluvium from an unknown fungus in the stones poisoned the air? Or a man-made gas, some sort of nerve gas intended to kill him? And those extraordinary scenes in the chambers—had they really happened? First, the old hag chained to the stone pillar, moaning and wailing and calling his name. Then the weird kiss, the chains falling off as if by magic, accompanied by a clap of thunder. The musty scent, the parchmentlike skin. Yes, he could remember all that.

And that second scene of the room ablaze with candles and flowers. And that fantastic transformation from hag to beauty . . . he could still hear her laughter and her soft voice whispering, "one more step, precious man. One more step, lover." Then the pitch into space and the cold water of the moat. He could recall his last thought as he hit the water—never trust a witch.

It was all like the old legend. He had freed the witch of Hanta with a kiss and given back what his ancestor had taken away three hundred years before—her freedom, her youth, and her beauty. Had it all been a dream, a drug-induced hallucination? He had a fantastic thought. Had this been the true purpose behind the plague of vampires, all the scares, the attacks, the murders? All arranged by the ancient, chained witch to draw him from the Skull Cave in the Deep Woods—to lure him thousands of miles into the decaying cellars of Hanta to free her with a kiss? He shook himself. A ridiculous notion.

He lay back and rested in the grass, breathing deeply of the fresh night air as strength flowed back into his body and his head cleared. It all had to be a kind of drugged nightmare inspired by the old Phantom Chronicle and these ancient ruins. But wait, he told himself, those children of Piotr as well as others had claimed to have seen the witch in this place. Had they all gone through a similar drugged experience, or was it all imagination?

Now look, he told himself almost angrily, stop woolgathering and think straight. If there was some sort of nerve gas in the corridor, how did it get there. From fungus in the walls? Or man-made? And that earlier business in the torture chamber, the wax dummy in the coffin. Who had arranged that? And what on earth did vampires have to do with a witch? That combination had always puzzled him. What had happened to Chief Peta after he fled? Was he back in his office gulping brandy? If so, he might have told the story to his angry aide, Sergeant Malo, which would bring him roaming about in the ruins. Too many questions. It was time to get back into the ruins and get some answers. He started to get to his feet, feeling automatically for his guns in their holsters. The guns were gone.

Had they fallen into the moat when he fell? Possibly. They were not held too tightly in the holsters in order to permit a fast draw. Whatever was waiting inside these ruins, it would be wiser to have his guns back. He must try to find them. He still had his slim flashlight. He turned on the narrow beam briefly to find the marks on the muddy shore where Devil had dragged him from the water. As the wolf watched, he stepped into the dark water at this point. There was a steep drop-off. He looked up and could see the opening in the wall from which he had fallen. This would be the place. He dove into the water, remembering his ancestor's words about the moat, "swarming with various small and loathsome things, some with tentacles. . . His ancestor had "dispatched several bolder creatures with my dagger . . The Phantom still had his knife, tucked in his boot, and drew it in case he was attacked. But nothing came his way. Perhaps by this time, nothing survived in the old moat.

He dove down some ten or twelve feet below the surface and explored the muddy bottom with his hands. Though he found many objects—bottles, pieces of carved stone, some metal utensils perhaps of another age, and other things the nature of which he could not guess—there were no guns. He made repeated attempts, but in vain. As he felt about in the muck, he moved a heavy stone. Some material or fabric that was under the stone floated up.

He finally returned to the surface, giving up the search. Possibly in the daylight, he could find the guns if they were there. But perhaps they weren't there at all. Had they fallen out in the room above? Or had the witch taken them? He remembered her brushing against him. He sat on the bank, soaking wet and chilled by the cold night air. He couldn't wait for daylight. What had to be done must be done quickly. The vampires, whoever they were, must know about him. They'd left the dummy and the lighted torches. They must have seen Chief Peta flee.

Some cloth was sticking to his wet leg, probably the stuff that had floated up from the bottom when he moved the stone. He pulled it off absently. It was nothing of interest to him. His mind was elsewhere. But there was something familiar about this stuff ... a certain rough wrinkled texture. And something else like grass or string. He hurriedly shone his light on the wet clump, then unfolded it and smoothed it out. For a moment, his mind reeled.

It was a kind of mask, the sort one might wear to a

costume party. It was a mask that covered the entire head like a sack, and it had long stringy white hair attached to it. Even in its collapsed, soaked condition, it was clearly the mask of an old woman with wrinkled yellowish grainy skin like parchment. The eyeholes were empty, but it was easy to visualize the glittering eyes behind them. It was the face of the ancient witch of Hanta.

CHAPTER 16

The Phantom felt such relief he almost laughed aloud. The world was making sense again. He had been weakened and drugged by some kind of gas. But the rest had been no dream. The "old witch" had been chained to the stone pillar, had shed her hag disguise and disgarded it in the moat, reappearing as the beautiful young vision. What a stunt! But why? Who was doing all this? Obviously, someone who knew the legend of the Phantom and the witch of Hanta. Someone who knew about the "blood-drinking demons" of that faraway time.

He was beginning to see the picture. Those men—Hans and the others from that big shiny car—trying to scare away the farmers and get their land cheaply, using the old superstitious fears of vampires for the purpose. That all appeared to be a fact, but it all seemed too easy. Big corporations, even unethical ones, did not ordinarily use such weird methods. They had more normal ways of persuasion such as mortgages, foreclosures, or the simple roughhouse tactics of hired goons. Why all this vampire mumbo-jumbo? And why create such fear of the witch of Hanta-Hunda. Was it to keep people away from these ruins? How did that fit in with the land grabbers? Too many questions. . . It was time to find some answers.

He got up and walked along the moat, looking for a stone

path across it. Devil moved silently at his side. As he reached the pile of stones that served as a bridge, there was a shot. A bullet whizzed past near him. Instantly, he dropped to the ground. Devil flattened in the grass. The Phantom was not hit, but he was outraged. He knew that sound. The bullet had been from one of his own guns. They were not in the muck at the bottom of the moat. All of his diving and probing in that filthy water had been wasted. The "witch" had taken his guns. He had a memory of that beautiful young face as he had last seen her. Were his guns in her hands now?

He watched the full moon as it traveled silently across the sky. There was a bank of clouds ahead, and the moon sailed into them like a galleon into a fog. The sky darkened. He jumped to his feet and sped over the bridge into the ruins. Two more shots whizzed close as he ducked behind a broken wall. Whoever was shooting was no beginner. Even in the dark and at a gallop, those bullets had barely missed him.

He crawled along the broken wall, Devil following closely. From the direction of the gunshots, he knew he had cover here. The night remained dark as he ran in a crouch from wall to boulder to pillar to rock heap. For one moment, the moon revealed him by peeking through the cloud cover, and once more the gun fired, hitting the stone two inches above his head. How infuriating to be hunted with his own gun! His faithful weapon that had served him so well in numerous tight spots. It was almost as if it had betrayed him. He grinned at that thought. I'd better get this whole business settled, he told himself, before I go balmy, blaming my gun.

He was near the front of the ruins, where he had first entered. In the distance on the roads, in that same patch of moonlight, he saw the little jalopy of Chief Peta parked, it seemed, ages ago. Then the chief had not driven away. In his panic, had he not stopped to get in the car? The Phantom thought back. Yes, he had given the ignition key to him when they got out. Or had the chief failed to escape from the ruins? That was a worrisome thought. Had they caught him?

He reached the old stone staircase and went down to the iron door. It was half-open. Whoever was tending this place had grown careless. Or maybe they were no longer worried about visitors. He moved silently down the familiar dark corridor, passed the cell that served as his hideout, and went on toward the light that now flickered in the distance. As he and Devil approached the torture chamber, they heard voices. Several mocking, one desperate. There seemed to be no effort at secrecy now. The place was wide-open. He peered around a corner to look into the big chamber and was astonished at the scene.

There were a half-dozen men dressed in the black outfits of the vampires—capes, big broad hats, kerchiefs masking their eyes, fangs protruding from their lips. A half-dozen torches burned on the walls. The black-clad figures were crowded about a device. It was the big metal and wood frame known as the rack. Lying flat on his back on the tilted frame was Chief Ivor Peta.

His hands were tied by the wrists to a cylinder above his head. His legs were tied by the ankles to a cylinder below his feet. One of the black-clad figures was slowly, inch by inch, turning a big wheel that revolved the two cylinders. The effect of this was to stretch the victim, in this case Chief Peta. This torture device, a relic of the Middle Ages, had been used by inquisitors in many nations to extract information. If the stretching continued, the arms and legs were pulled out of their joints—a most horrible and painful torture ending in death. The black-clad figures were using the old device for its old purpose.

"Who was Mr. Walker?" said one in a heavy, guttural voice.

"I don't know. I told you I don't know," cried Chief Peta in pain.

"Don't lie. He came from that place, Bangalla. Why?"

"I don't know."

"Did you send for him?"

"No, no, I never heard of him."

"Do you know Walker is not his name?"

"No, no. Stop!"

"We won't stop until you tell us the truth."

"I told you."

"You told us nothing. Stop faking or we'll pull you apart," said the spokesman brutally. "Do you know what Mr. Walker is called?"

"Called?"

"What does the word Phantom mean to you?"

"Phantom? Ghost?"

"The truth, Peta, the truth."

The black-clad man at the wheel gave the crank another turn and Peta screamed in agony. The Phantom had heard enough.

In three huge strides, he was among them, his iron fists flailing like triphammers. His sudden appearance caused an uproar. Some of the black-clad figures fled at the first sight of him. Others tried to fight, drawing long knives or guns. His first target was the spokesman. Next the man at the crank. Both fell like stones. Bones cracked as he flung two more men against the stone wall. Suddenly, the shouting and panic was over. There were groans from the fallen men, moans from Peta, and the sound of distant running feet.

With quick slices of his knife, the Phantom freed Peta and

helped him off the rack. He had reached him in time. No bones were broken. But the chief was exhausted and trembling.

"They caught me before I could . . . before I could . . ."

"Before you could get away."

"Yes. What were those devils doing to me?"

"Stretching you on an old torture instrument."

"All about you. Why do they—do they—?"

"Care?"

"Yes."

'We'll find out, Chief Peta. Right now, let's find out who they are."

He pulled off the hat, kerchief, and fangs of the heavyset spokesman. The chief stared at him.

"Why, that's Gunda, my third cousin."

Gunda was the proprietor of the tavern. He'd felt the Phantom's fist the night before.

"Your third cousin. Hmm, blood is thicker than water; evidently, it is not thicker than dirt."

"Dirt?"

"Land or whatever these hoodlums are after. Let's have a look at this dandy. He was turning the crank, stretching you. He seemed to enjoy it. I heard him. Want to guess who he is?"

Peta stared with wide eyes as the Phantom removed the hat, kerchief, and fangs of the rack operator.

"Sergeant Malo!" said Peta in utter amazement.

Malo was conscious. He stared at them with angry eyes and obscenities dribbled like bile from his mouth.

"Yes, surprised me too. I thought he was just nasty. He's certainly that, but he's also involved with this gang."

"Gang? What gang?"

"That's what we have to find out. Is Malo related to you, too?"

"Him? No," said Peta, contemptuous toward his assistant for the first time. "He's not even froni Koqania. He's a foreigner," he added, with all the scorn of a man whose people had lived in the same valley for a thousand years.

"And you made him your assistant?"

"He had good training. He was an officer in the military police of his country. We are farmers here. Such experience is rare," said Peta. Now that he was sober and over his fear, the Phantom saw that Ivor Peta was no fool, but a solid man trying to do his job.

Peta seemed to read his thoughts.

"I guess I looked like an idiot to you. I'm not a drinker, not used to it and couldn't hold it. But all this business had me out of my mind."

The Phantom nodded. "We're not to the bottom of all this business yet."

"I was going to ask you what in damnation this is all about."

"I've got some ideas, but not the entire answer. Let's wait until we get more facts."

Peta nodded. "I still don't know who you are and why you're here."

"Does a name or a reason matter as long as we get the job done?"

During this talk, Malo had been recovering from the painful punches. The men had their backs to him. He suddenly leaped to his feet and dashed off. The Phantom turned and Devil started after him.

"Hold, Devil."

"Hey, we can't let him get away!" shouted Peta.

"I want to see where he goes. These cellars go on forever. Maybe he can show the way."

"To what?"

"That's the big question. Watch these men." Gunda and another black-clad figure were still on the floor. "One of them had a gun. Here it is." He picked it up and handed it to the chief. "If they try to get away—or if anyone comes—use it."

"You want me to wait here?" said Peta in dismay.

"No. When they come to, take them to town. Put them behind bars. Then come back in daylight. Maybe we'll have more customers for you."

"There seem to be lots of them. You going to handle this alone!"

"Yes."

The Phantom started off.

"Wait," said Peta, suddenly anxious. "What good is this gun? I told you I fired five shots and didn't hurt them."

"You think your third cousin Gunda is a vampire? Think the bullets would hurt him?"

"Yes, but—"

The Phantom took a slug from his pouch.

"I took this from your gun when I was in your office. It remained after you fired off the other five." He tossed it to Peta.

"That's a blank," said Peta.

"So were the other five. That's why they didn't kill. Didn't even tickle."

"But how?"

"Your assistant, Sergeant Malo, fixed that. He's been in on this thing since the beginning."

Peta breathed deeply.

"Blanks? Well, I'll be damned."

"Okay now?"

Peta nodded. "If one of those mugs shows his ugly snout here. I'll blank him!"

The Phantom smiled. "Good man. We'll go now."

"Say, Malo's been in what thing since the beginning?"

"That's what we have to find out."

"You let him get a big lead on you. How you going to find him?"

The Phantom picked up the hat and kerchief he'd taken from Malo and put them under Devil's nose. Devil sniffed, then started off. The Phantom trotted after him. In a moment, they were gone in the dark corridor.

Peta examined the gun, which was loaded with real cartridges. Gunda and the other man were stirring. He pulled off the hat, kerchief, and fangs of the second man. He was a stranger. Both were grunting and coughing, waking up. The chief looked at them closely. Something on their jaws. Like a death's head. Malo had one like that from that night in the office. Left there by the right fist of Mr. Walker. Peta had noticed the ring on that hand—a death's head ring. Mr. Walker? He still didn't know who he was, or why he was here. Did it matter? What had he said? "Does a name or a reason matter as long as we get the job done?"

"Hey, you two, get on your feet," said Chief Ivor Peta.

CHAPTER 17

Now master and wolf moved through the maze of underground tunnels. Both traveled as silently as if they floated through the air, Devil on his footpads, the Phantom on his soft leather soles. Silence was necessary. There was no light in this area, but rather utter blackness. They could be ambushed at any moment. The tunnels dipped and rose, rising and falling to various levels. In some places, the ceilings were so low that he had to follow on hands and knees. In one place, he wriggled on his belly after the wolf. This was a distant area of the subterranean ruins that he had never visited. In places, they crawled through the icy water of underground streams. Often, Devil hesitated before a fork in their route, then his nose picked up the scent. This pursuit would have been impossible without his sharp hunter's nose.

As they crawled on the rock or dirt floor, or edged along narrow, barely passable areas, soft hairy things crawled over his bare hands. Once a lizardlike creature, brushed from the low ceiling by the Phantom's head, dropped to his shoulder and crawled around his neck before being swept to the ground. He could imagine the little animal bom and bred in this place without light, blind like creatures of the caverns. He wished he could turn on his light to inspect the surroundings as they moved. Some of the walls and floors were as smooth as marble. On some, he felt intricate carvings while some were rough stone; all probably were the work of builders who lived centuries apart. No one knew the Origin of this Hanta castle or its age. Some said it dated back to before The Flood.

He was still without his guns, but he carried his knife in one hand. That and his hard fists were a match for almost any weapon. He moved now with a growing sense of excitement, for he felt that the truth about this place was near. Several times they stopped, hearing the distant murmur of voices coming through layers of rock, then went on, ducking low overhangs, crawling, climbing, edging through narrow passes. Sergeant Malo must have known this route by heart. Perhaps as he fled, he had used a flashlight. Now they began to hear other sounds, sounds he had heard before, wheezing, whirring, rasping. Faint at first, then louder as they approached what must be the source of these sounds. Now they were especially loud at his right hand. He moved on. The sounds became fainter. He moved back. The sound increased. He paused where the sound was loudest and felt the wall with his hands. This was a smooth area, made of marble or a similar polished stone. In this utter darkness, his fingers found a vertical crack in the wall, a crack that rose about four feet above the ground. At the top of the crack, he felt a horizontal crack running off it for several feet. Excited, he got to his knees and found what he was hoping to find—a horizontal crack parallel to the one above, running along the base of the wall. It was a doorway flush in the stone wall.

Using his knife, he tried to pry it open. To his delight it yielded, and as the crack widened a pale light shone through from inside. Now he was able to get his fingers into the crack, and he slowly pulled it open. The low stone door, for that is what it was, swung open silently on well- oiled hinges. And through the open doorway came the pale light and the loud sounds of whirring, wheezing, and rasping. Whatever it meant, this was the place.

Before entering, he peered into it. It seemed to be a huge chamber carved out of a natural cave. Low-power lights were set in the ceiling which also held a network of pipes and wires. There were rows of slim crates of various sizes on platforms, all stacked on end, each separated from the others by uprights. And in the dim background, far beyond the rows of crates, there were several large metallic boxes. The sounds came from them. That was all he had time to take in, for as he crawled through the low entrance, Devil gave a soft warning growl.

The Phantom was instantly alert, trying to cover the entire cavern in a sweeping glance. He saw nothing, but there had to be something. Devil had sensed it. He looked up. Above his head, seated on a ledge, was a figure in black staring down at him—a "vampire" without the fangs and kerchief. There was a look of amazement on his brutish face as he stared at the masked man kneeling a few feet below him.

The guard, if that was what he was, uttered a sharp cry, then picked up a long knife from the ledge and dove at the kneeling man. His action was intended to land him on the intruder's back, following which he could plunge the knife into him. But the plan failed, because when he landed the intruder was no longer there. He had moved, with blinding speed, and the guard hit the rocky floor with a thump. There was a second thump—more of a crunch—as something that felt as hard as the stone floor crashed against his jaw. It might have been an iron bar or a boulder. It was, in fact, the Phantom's fist. The man collapsed. The entire action had lasted only a few seconds. The Phantom was still on his knees. Devil peered in at the low entrance. The whirring, wheezing, and rasping continued. The man had cried out. Had he been heard?

Suddenly, the whirring, wheezing, and rasping from those big metallic boxes stopped. The chamber was silent. He touched Devil's jaws, and both man and animal held their breaths for a short time. This was a trick he had taught the wolf long before. They listened for sounds of any other breathing in the room. If there was any, it was inaudible. Then with a clank, the noise from the boxes started up again. He studied the sound, trying to guess the purpose of those boxes and the machinery in them causing the sounds. Something else to find out—but first, he wanted to look into the lines of wooden crates. What did they contain?

He crossed quietly to the first row for a closer look. There was nothing antique about them. Impossible to guess how long they'd been there, but they were modern crates. He lifted one slightly. It was about five feet square, a foot thick, and surprisingly light. There were letters and a number painted neatly on one side: DV-1. He lowered the crate back to its base. All the crates were on wooden platforms raised about a foot from the rocky floor. To protect them from flooding, rats, or what? He examined another oblong crate, also lightweight, also neatly numbered: R-1. Next to it, a larger one: MA-1. Glancing about the room, he estimated there must be several hundred crates in a variety of sizes. Most of them were tied with wire. What was inside?

This entire mystery reminded him of those Chinese puzzle boxes. You manage to open one and there is another one inside. You open that to find a smaller one, and on and on. Solve one puzzle in Koqania and another appeared. From land-grabbing vampires (were they really interested in farming?) to a corrupt policeman, to a playacting witch (what was she up to?). And now these crates and the noisy machinery in the metal boxes. Chinese puzzles, indeed. The only solution was to open the boxes.

He selected the crate marked DV-1 and, without touching it, examined it. It was one of the few without wire tied about it. This would be no simple job. The crate was solid and well made, put together with dozens of screws and nails. As he was about to lift the crate, the big metallic boxes started up again with a clank. He walked over to them, curious about them. The machinery inside was completely enclosed. Several large ducts protruded from the back and were built up along the walls and across the ceiling. At regular intervals, there were grills in the ducts. He put his hand over one. Air flowed out. Of course. These contained some sort of air-conditioning machinery. The rest of the cellars were damp and cold. This room was dry and pleasant. Another Chinese puzzle box. Solving one mystery only revealed a new one. Why would anyone install elaborate and expensive air conditioning in the ancient ruins of Koqania? One didn't have to be a genius to conclude it involved the crates.

He returned to the one he had selected and lifted it carefully out of its wooden cradle. Somewhere in the distance, a bell rang. He stood motionless, listening, then quickly examined the cradle of the crate with his small flashlight. There was a fine wire running along the side. It was broken, one end dangling. Had he broken it in lifting the crate out? Had he set off that bell, a burglar alarm? He got the answer swiftly as all the lights in the chamber went off and he was in complete darkness.

He heard soft sounds in the dark, whispers and footsteps. He lowered himself into a crouch. Whoever had turned off the lights, unless the system was automatic, had probably observed him through a peephole and knew where he was. So it would be wise to move. As he took a step, Devil taking one step at his side, a powerful flashlight beam suddenly blazed out of the darkness, directed at his head, momentarily blinding him.

"Don't move, Mr. Walker," said a familiar voice.

It was the voice of Sergeant Malo. The Phantom shaded his eyes with his hand. Near the air-conditioning machines, he could make out the dark figure of the corrupt cop.

"Don't move, or I'll shoot you through the head," continued the cold, vicious voice. He is a nasty fellow, thought the Phantom.

"Don't get so excited, Malo. You know I have no guns."

"Yes, I know that. You might be interested to know I am holding one of them aimed at your head."

Only one? Who had the other one, he wondered?

"You hit me twice, you—!" said Malo, using a vicious Koqania oath that stung the Phantom.

"I didn't hit you hard enough, Malo. The third time I will."

The man behind the flashlight laughed.

"There won't be a third time, you—"

There was whispering in the darkness behind Malo. Evidently someone was hidden behind the air conditioners.

"I'm handling this," snapped Malo, evidently answering the whisperer. "Now I want you to answer a question."

"Nothing could make me happier," said the Phantom.

"What?"

"What's your question?"

"You hit me twice, once on each side of my jaw. That left two marks, is that not so?"

"It sounds possible."

"Possible? You—! They look like death's heads."

"That's what they are."

"I can't get them off. I've rubbed, I've scrubbed, I've used everything—even pumice stone. They don't come off."

The Phantom chuckled. His mark was similar to a tattoo, but even more indelible.

"That's tough, Malo," he said.

"You think it's funny! Answer me! How do I get it off?"

"Simple. Remove the skin."

The flashlight wavered. The Phantom could estimate the man's rage. Angry men didn't shoot as straight as calm ones.

"You idiot! Say your prayers. I'm going to kill you," said Malo, shouting. His voice echoed in this cave.

"No, Malo," said another voice sharply. It was a new voice to the Phantom. From its tone, a voice used to command. "Not here."

Malo actually growled at that. Devil, crouched behind the Phantom, answered with a soft growl of his own. The Phantom had considered launching Devil at the gunman, but didn't want to risk the animal's getting shot.

Not there. Why not here? Obviously, because of the crates. The mysterious crates. Afraid of damaging them?

"Not here, Malo," repeated the commanding voice, and Malo grunted acquiescence, a Koqania equivalent of okay. There was another whispered exchange, probably about where to take him.

"Stand up and come toward me slowly," said Malo, and the Phantom could imagine him talking between clenched teeth. "No tricks, Walker, or whoever you are, or you die right here."

No, indeed, thought the Phantom. Nobody's going to start shooting here. Not here.

The crate that he had removed was leaning against an upright at his side. As he arose, he suddenly grabbed it and placed it in front of him as a shield. Without pausing, he rushed toward the flashlight and Malo.

As the Phantom moved behind his lightweight wooden

shield, he sensed that Malo was about to shoot despite orders.

The shot never came. The commanding voice cried out, "No, Malo! It's DV-1." Malo answered that with another oath, then screamed. The light fell from his hand and broke on the hard floor, throwing the room into darkness. Somewhere behind the silent machines, an iron door clanked shut. As if on cue, the air conditioners whirred on. Still holding the crate as a shield, the Phantom stopped short. Malo was lying only a few feet ahead in the darkness. He groaned and choked and was silent.

The Phantom listened for the sound of his breathing, but the machines just behind him were loud enough to drown it out. Then the machines stopped, evidently operated by thermostats. Now the chamber was silent.

He touched Devil's nose and once more the man and animal held their breaths and listened. No one in the chamber was breathing. He flipped on his flashlight. In its narrow beam, he saw Malo. He was lying on his side of the floor, still dressed in his black vampire outfit. A long knife protruded from his back. Koqania police department's Sergeant Malo was dead.

CHAPTER 18

The Phantom was shocked and angered by the sight. Death is never pretty; murder is always ugly. Nothing could be more brutal than stabbing a colleague in the back. What had caused this vicious action? There had been whispered advice, consultations, then a command, then the decision—death. Malo had been about to shoot through the crate, through DV-1. That cost him his life. Who had wielded the long knife? The owner of the commanding voice? So it seemed. Why? What could DV-1 contain to cause such an instant decision to murder in cold blood? And in a way despised throughout history as cowardly and repugnant—stabbing a man in the back?

All these thoughts flashed through his mind as he examined Malo quickly to see if anything could be done for him. Lying next to the slain man was a gun, the Phantom's. He quickly took it and ran to the iron door. It had an ordinary lock which snapped into place when the door was shut. He took a quick look back at the crate standing against the upright. On a hunch he ran back, took the crate, and hid it behind the air conditioners. Then he returned to the iron door. He held his gun close to the lock and shattered it with a shot.

The room on the other side of the door, a small cellar, was softly lit. There was no one in it. It was furnished with a desk, chairs, couch, a small wooden cabinet, and a green metal file cabinet. He looked quickly through the desk, searching for information. The drawers were empty. He turned to the file cabinet. It was locked. He was tempted to blow it open, but it could wait. The little wooden cabinet contained bottles and several glasses. Whiskey, gin, vodka, and the local brandy. The furniture was the kind seen in modern offices. This could be the private office of an executive. In that case, it should have a private bathroom. He opened a side door and smiled. It did.

Almost as incredible as the vampires, the torture devices, the witch before and after, DV-1, and the murder of Sergeant Malo was this office. So ordinary, so everyday, so like countless other little offices in cities all over the world to be found here in the ancient ruins of Koqania, and the modern bathroom—much more out of place in this setting than the medieval torture chamber. There was another door at the side, evidently the exit. It was closed and locked with a lock similar to the first. He guessed that one key opened both doors. The wielder of the knife had gone through this room, and out that door. Perhaps he had not been alone; others could have gone with him.

The Phantom was in no great hurry to pursue him, not with the crates in the next room. If DV-1 was worth killing a fellow worker to save, how about all the rest? They would not go far. He was filled with curiosity about those crates, anxious to open at least one. What could they contain? Drags, weapons, jewels, military or industrial secrets? He would have to wait to find out.

He would also wait until they, whoever they were, returned. Doubtlessly, they were outside this room somewhere, preparing traps or ambushes, waiting for him to pursue them, knowing he would be armed now with his own gun. It amused him to sit in the swivel chair and put his feet on the desk like a proper executive. His gun was in his lap, ready as he watched both exit doors. Devil sat at his side.

As he sat, he thought of the beautiful young "witch." Where was she? The villagers seemed to regard her as the leader of the "vampires." His guess was that she was part of the group, and the real leader was the man with the commanding voice. So he sat and meditated, seemingly relaxed and idle, but his eyes were sharp and his body tense and ready. They would tire of their traps and ambushes soon, and come back to look for him. At this point, the Phantom was making only one mistake. This executive room was the trap.

"Don't move, don't turn, or you are a dead man," said a now-familiar voice behind him. The Phantom obeyed. It was the same voice that had commanded, "Not here."

"Now throw your gun across the room."

He looked regretfully at his polished weapon. He had recovered it for such a short time.

"Do you mind if I don't throw it, and risk breaking it?"

"You'll not use it again," said the voice with a touch of amusement in the tone. "I want it out of your reach."

"Mind if I let my friend put it over there?"

"Your friend?"

The Phantom glanced at Devil.

"If that is possible, why not? I must warn you, there are two rifles aimed at your head."

The Phantom clicked his tongue. Instantly, Devil was on his feet. The Phantom held the gun out by the barrel. Devil took it in his teeth. The Phantom pointed to the far wall. Devil walked slowly to the wall with the gun in his jaws, looking back at his master as he went.

"Place," said the Phantom. Wish I'd taught him to shoot, he thought.

Devil lowered the gun to the floor, then trotted back happily to receive a pat.

There were several amused laughs from behind.

"Bravo," said the speaker.

At the top of the far wall, near the ceiling, a small panel slid open. A face, then a gun barrel, appeared. A second panel opened, then another face and gun appeared. The Phantom looked behind him. There were two panels open. In one, another face and gun barrel. The second panel was empty. Had the speaker been in that one? After a moment of quiet, broken only by the heavy breathing of the faces in the panels, the outer door opened. A man carrying a pistol stepped in. Behind him were two husky black-clad men, each with rifles. The first man looked familiar. He was an elegant looking gray-haired man in expensive business clothes, and as he faced the desk and adjusted a monocle in his right eye, the Phantom remembered. The man had been with Sergeant Malo that night in the tavern.

"Stand up and face the wall," he said sharply. Devil looked quickly at his master. He recognized the hostile tone. The Phantom shook his head. He did as he was ordered, standing up, facing the wall. One of the husky black-clad riflemen quickly frisked him, finding the knife, which he took.

"Turn around."

He did so. The monocled man faced him with an arrogant look on his haughty face. A rifleman stood at either side. Above, in the wall, were the riflemen peering through the panels.

"You are still alive because we spent a good deal of time and money trying to find out who you are, and all we learned was confusing. Who are you? Why are you here?"

"May I ask you the same question?"

"Our time is short. We have no time for games. You will answer my questions." His tone was sharp, a military commander giving orders in the field.

"Very well. I came to find the vampires and the witch. I found them. Or shall I say they found me?"

"You have not answered my question."

"I came to find the vampires and the witch, to destroy them. Is that better?"

"Better. Is there any other reason?"

What other reason could he have? He thought for a moment, then tried a shot in the dark.

"To get DV-1 and perhaps R-2 and MA-2 and FH-4 as well."

That was a bombshell. The monocle dropped from his eye. For a moment, he lost his sneering expression and gaped. The others looked at each other in astonishment.

"How do you know about these things," the spokesman stammered.

"I was told."

All three men took a step toward him, weapons raised, "Who told you?"

This was almost farcical. He didn't have the slightest idea what he was talking about, but obviously had touched raw nerves. Might as well play the game further, using someone who couldn't be hurt by it now.

"Sergeant Malo told me."

That really hit them. They stared at each other, then at him.

"He's lying," said one of the men.

"Ask him," said the Phantom calmly.

"See if he can still talk," said the spokesman coldly. Evidently, after the knife thrust, they hadn't waited to see if it had finished him. A man left and returned quickly.

"No," he said.

"I don't put it past that little upstart," snarled the elegant man, losing his smoothness for the moment. "Let's say he told you—tell us what he told you."

The Phantom looked at him quietly. The spokesman's steely eyes became narrow and cold.

"We can make men talk," he said.

"No doubt. I've already taken DV-1," he said.

This caused exclamations from all of them. A man ran into

the big room where the crates were, and returned after a moment, breathless.

"Not there. It's gone," he shouted.

The men looked at the spokesman. It was clear that he was their leader. Now his face was grim and cruel.

"Remember the torture room? The Rack. And there are other refinements. Shall we use them?"

"I wouldn't recommend it," said the Phantom casually, his mind working fast. "DV-1 is not only hidden. It is prepared."

"Meaning what?"

"A small time-bomb attachment. If it's not turned off, it will destroy it and whatever else is within a hundred feet of it."

The leader turned pale.

"When? When?" he shouted, his aplomb gone.

The Phantom smiled and remained silent.

"Do you have any idea what DV-1 is worth?" the man cried.

The Phantom nodded. He didn't have the slightest notion, but it was obviously worth a great deal to these men. "Did you come here to cut in on this—to hijack us."

"I wouldn't say that."

"What would you say? You want a piece of this deal?"

"If I were in your position, that's what I would think."

"You've got a time bomb ticking, we can't stand here chatting. What's your deal?"

"Why get so excited. If DV-1 goes, there's always R-2 or MA-1."

"You bloody fool. Are you mad? Or trying to joke with me? Name your deal. Name your cut!"

Cut was a good word for these cutthroats, he told himself.

"Where is she?" he said.

The change in subject confused them. "She?"

"The witch of Hanta."

"That's none of your business."

"Ah, but it is. The lady tried to kill me."

"Nonsense. She was playing a game."

"She played it well. I found her quite beautiful. She is part of the deal."

The spokesman stared at him. One of the other men grinned.

"Deal!"

"She will be part of my 'cut.' I want her," said the Phantom.

The spokesman's face became livid. He clenched his fist and he raised his pistol.

"Hey, Colonel, easy. Remember DV-1," said the man at his right. The leader, the colonel, glared at him, then at the Phantom.

"Leave her out of this, understood?"

The Phantom nodded. He had learned what he wanted to know. The girl was part of the gang and was the leader's wife or sweetheart. And the leader had the title or rank of colonel. His military bearing was real.

"Let's get down to business," said the colonel.

"Not with guns in my face."

The colonel put his pistol in a shoulder holster. At his nod, the other two leaned their rifles against the wall.

"And them," said the Phantom pointing to the two riflemen watching from the wall panels.

"They stay as they are," said the colonel sharply. "Now talk."

The Phantom's head was buzzing with all the questions about these men and their secrets. But since he was presumed to know the answers, he couldn't ask the questions, at least not yet.

"How much time on that timer for the bomb?" said the colonel.

"Enough," said the Phantom.

"He could be lying about that," said one of the men, a husky who looked like an ex-prizefighter—smashed nose, cauliflower ears, and all.

"Lying?" said the Phantom, smiling "You want to wait and see?"

"No!" shouted the colonel. "Get on with it."

He stood by the edge of the desk and considered his next move. Two barrels were pointed at him from high up on the wall. The room was lighted by a single large bulb that hung over the front of the desk, a foot or so above his head. His plan of action formed in a flash. (In the jungle, quick decisions mean life or death.) He began to talk, a rambling chat that skirted the edge of the secrets.

"I cannot make an overall arrangement. It is necessary to get down to cases—to crates—to be more specific in each case as to value. After all, DV-1 and the others are not easily disposable." The colonel nodded. That was an easy guess. If they were easily disposable, why go to all the trouble to hide them here, whatever they were?

As he spoke, he gestured with his hands. This was not his usual behavior, but he had observed tradesmen doing this when they bargained with each other in the town markets. So he waved his hands and arms in small movements at first, then broader ones as he seemed to warm to his subject. "And the very difficulty of disposability increases our mutual risk and makes the return more subject to other obligations which might be costly, but at the same time necessary to effectuate a reasonable return on our efforts."

As he spoke, he saw that they watched closely, trying to

make sense out of his rambling discourse but mainly remaining patient until he got to the point. The main question he knew, was not how much of a cut he wanted. It was DV-1, the missing crate. They hadn't looked very hard. Obviously, it was so valuable that they assumed if one hid it, one would hide it in a very secret place—not only a few feet away on the other side of the wall behind the air conditioner. He also knew they would agree to any terms he suggested for his share. And once they had DV-1 safely in their hands, they would kill him.

As he rambled, their eyes became slightly glazed with boredom, waiting for him to get to the point and shut up. The men above in the wall panels yawned, letting their rifles droop. Meanwhile, his hands waving and gesticulating, and as the colonel glanced away, indicating boredom, the Phantom's hand flew up and smashed the light bulb. The room was suddenly in pitch darkness.

The sleepy atmosphere of the room was suddenly charged with shouts and cries. Then two shots exploded from the watching riflemen, aimed at where the masked man had been. But he was no longer there. In one step, he had flattened the colonel, who fell to the floor with a grunt. Then he moved to the other two who, after their surprise, had time only to make a step toward their rifles at the wall. They never got there. An iron fist, lashing out of the darkness, dropped one, then the other, as effectively as if they had been hit with baseball bats. They dropped without a sound.

The two riflemen up on a ledge outside the room dared not shoot into the darkness again. Even that first shot had been risky. They might have hit their own men. They stared into the darkness, trying to see something. They heard crunching sounds (the Phantom's fist) and the noise of bodies hitting the floor. Then they hurriedly started down the ladders that stood against the ledge, when suddenly they fell headlong into the air.

Racing out of the office, the Phantom kicked the ladders out from under them. They fell hard on the rocky floor. One landed on his head and stayed there. The other one started to his feet, but was bowled over by a hard fist that put him back on the floor with his companion. The Phantom was taking no chances against these odds. He was hitting hard. They would remain as they were for quite a while.

He returned to the office. There was no light there as he crossed to the crate-chamber door. He'd noticed a switch on the wall. He pulled it down and opened the door. The soft light filled the crate room once again. Light from the doorway entered the office. The two huskies were on their backs, knocked out. The colonel was on his knees, crawling weakly toward the rifles at the wall. The Phantom grabbed him by the collar of his expensive jacket and pulled him to his feet. He had been hit with less force and had regained consciousness. He was swearing softly in a foreign tongue. The Phantom half-led, half-dragged him toward the lighted crate chamber.

"Come, Colonel. We're going to open a few crates and get some answers," he said.

The colonel mumbled and struggled ineffectually. They got inside the big chamber, near the air-conditioning machines which were quiet for the moment. The colonel slumped to his knees.

"No, no," he said. "Don't kill me."

"You wanted to see DV-1? Here it is, Colonel."

The man was sitting on the floor by now, and the Phantom dragged him toward the air-conditioner box, then leaned behind it and pulled out the crate.

"Here it is, safe and sound. Now, open it."

"Don't kill me," repeated the colonel, terrified, barely hearing the masked man's words.

"It's DV-1. Open it, Colonel."

"Don't kill me. Take it. Take them all," he said. Again, still sitting on the ground.

"Are you kidding?" said a soft voice.

The Phantom's hand darted to his gun, but it wasn't there.

It was still in the office on the floor. There was a sudden shot, almost deafening in this cavern, and a bullet came within inches of his head. It ricocheted against the wall and hit an overhead pipe with a clang.

"I tried to miss. Next time, I won't miss," said the soft voice.

He knew the sound of that shot. It had come from his second, missing gun. And without seeing her, he knew who held it: the witch of Hanta-Hunda.

CHAPTER 19

"Turn this way. Put down that crate. Then put up your hands," commanded the soft voice. He did as he was told, placing the crate on the floor so that it rested against his leg. In the shadows cast by the pale light, he could see the outline of a head between a row of crates. As he put his hands in the air above his head, she stepped out into full view.

She was no longer the witch of Hanta with the shimmering gown and the long flowing blonde hair. Now her hair was red and stylishly short. In a tight knit shirt of deep green and the shortest possible miniskirt that revealed long legs like those of a ballerina, she was a striking figure. Brilliant jewels of green and white—emeralds and diamonds?—glittered in her earrings, in a double-strand necklace, and in a dozen rings on her fingers. She wore high, tight, black boots that matched a wide black belt glittering with jewels about her waist—striking and beautiful, but with the beauty of the tiger or the cobra before it strikes. Her red lips were not smiling now, and her gray eyes were hard.

"Hermann, get up and stop whimpering," she snapped. The colonel, still sitting on the floor, flushed and climbed to his feet.

"I wasn't whimpering," he whined.

The Phantom looked at him in surprise. This commanding figure, this military leader, was suddenly reduced in size. He turned to the Phantom and started for him.

"This—!" he said, using a string of foreign obscenities.

"Don't get in my way, Hermann," she shouted. "I don't want to shoot through you!"

The colonel jumped back quickly.

"Go ahead, shoot. Shoot the idiot!" he snarled.

"Not yet. We must learn more about this mysterious Mr. Walker from Bangalla. This Phantom."

"That was quite a performance you put on," said the Phantom.

"I thought I did it all quite well, didn't you, Hermann?" she said with a short humorless laugh.

"Why not, after all the rehearsals?" said Hermann.

"You never give me credit for anything," she said angrily. "How about you after all those rehearsals? Late with the thunder. And all you had to do was press a little button."

"It stuck. I'm not an engineer," he said loftily.

Thunder? The Phantom remembered that sound when he kissed the old witch. A sound tape. He listened to them curiously. Was she his wife, mistress, or boss? With his gun in her hand, pointing at him, he wanted to prolong the conversation.

"What was that gas out there in the corridor? It almost knocked me out," he said.

"Yes, Hermann, what about that gas? You said it was fatal," she said.

"It usually is, at least it was in experiments. It doesn't affect everyone the same way," he said irritably.

"You intended to kill me?" asked the Phantom.

"That was his intention," she said scornfully, waving the gun toward Hermann. He had opened a thin gold case and was nervously lighting a cigarette with a gold lighter.

"Don't smoke in here," she snapped.

He hurriedly stamped on his cigarette.

"Not your intention?" asked the Phantom.

"Not then," she said. "I wanted to wait, to find out more about you. But they overruled me. That's the last time that will happen," she snapped.

"They?" said the Phantom.

"Hermann and his stormtroopers," she said, again scornful. "His bully boys. You've met most of them. Are any of them still on their feet, Hermann?"

"Oh, shut up," he said peevishly.

"Do you mind telling me who you are?" said the Phantom.

She snorted. "Of course I mind. That's what I'm asking you."

"What difference does it make, Greta?" said Hermann. "Shoot him and be done with it."

"Shoot him and be done with it," she mocked. "How did you ever get to be a colonel with that brain? This man may have an organization behind him, and know more about us than we think."

"Impossible."

"Impossible? Look at his costume. Like the one in that old story. Why does he dress like that unless he knows?"

"What old story?" said the Phantom, fascinated.

" 'The Witch of Hanta and The Masked Stranger,' also called Phantom, as if you didn't know," she said. The gun, his gun, remained pointed at him.

"Greta," said the colonel, suddenly strong again. "I'm still in charge of this operation. I demand that you use that gun now, at once, on him."

"And who put you in charge" she shouted, angry.

"You know very well. The will named me," said the colonel.

"Who cares about that old paper now? You've made too many mistakes. You're too slow, too stupid."

"How dare you talk to me like that? Have you no respect?" shouted Hermann.

"You let Gerhart and those fools almost ruin our business. This is our business," she shouted, waving her gun at the crates. For the moment, yelling at each other, they had almost forgotten the Phantom. He chose that moment to pick up the crate and, holding it before him, dashed at the woman.

"Greta!" cried Hermann. "No—DV-1—don't shoot!"

She hesitated. Maybe the command did it, or the crate labeled DV-1. Whatever the cause, that moment's hesitation gave the Phantom the time he needed to cross to her. He drove the flat crate directly at her head so that she threw up her hands instinctively to protect her face. In a flash, the Phantom grasped her wrist as she fired. The bullet exploded into the rock ceiling. He dropped the crate, then twisted her wrist, forcing her to her knees. In the same movement, he took the gun away. It had all happened so quickly, Hermann had not moved. To Hermann and the woman called Greta, the Phantom moved unbelievably fast.

There was a moment of silence, broken only by the hard breathing of the man and the woman. Now it was her turn to whimper. She had fallen to her knees on the rocky floor and it hurt. Then she began to swear, producing foul language from such   beautiful lips.

"You idiot," she muttered at Hermann. "If you had shut up—"

"I'd be dead," said the Phantom.

"Correct," she said, getting to her feet.

"How many in your gang, outside of you two?"

They did not reply. She rubbed her knees and looked at Hermann.

"I want a cigarette," she said coldly.

"I asked you a question."

Hermann looked at him arrogantly, then folded his arms, saying without words, "Make me talk if you can."

Greta was more explicit with her string of obscenities.

The Phantom whistled softly. Devil came out of the darkness. Close to two hundred pounds and six feet from nose to tail, he seemed monstrous in this cavern. His long white fangs gleamed.

"Devil is a wolf. He is trained to kill his own meat. He is hungry. He will kill and eat what I tell him to kill and eat."

Hermann and Greta looked nervously at Devil. She tried to laugh.

"Expect us to believe that?"

"We are not fools," said Hermann.

The Phantom waved his gun toward Hermann.

"Go, Devil," he said.

Devil leaped at Hermann. Hermann screamed as the force of the leap knocked him to the floor. Devil stood over him, front paws on his chest, jaws open wide—wide enough to take in Hermann's whole head.

"No, no," he cried, terrified.

"Stop him," shouted Greta.

"Answer my question," said the Phantom.

"What question?" gasped Hermann, Devil's hot breath blowing in his face.

"How many in your gang?"

"Uh, thirteen. Get him off."

"Thirteen, counting you two?"

"What?" gasped Hermann, nearly fainting.

"Not counting us," said Greta, terrified too.

"Here, Devil."

The wolf left the fallen man and walked to his master, then turned so that his pale-blue eyes watched the man and woman. She started toward the man to help him get up.

"Stay where you are," said the Phantom. She stayed.

Thirteen, he thought. There had been the first man at the

church, then the two including the bartender Gunda, left in the torture chamber with Chief Peta, the guard here, Sergeant Malo, now dead, and the four riflemen in and about the office next door. That made nine. And two more, Hans and the fat one, left with Roko the farmer. That made eleven. Two left.

"Where are the others. Buying real estate?" said the Phantom.

Greta glared at him. The colonel got to his feet, and felt for his cigarette case.

"I'm waiting for the answer," said the Phantom.

The colonel looked quickly at Devil.

"Yes, buying real estate."

"Go on."

"A farmer up the valley, being stubborn."

"Like Roko."

"We have no interest in that real-estate idea. That was their idea, Gerhart and the others. They weren't satisfied," said Greta.

"They didn't have the imagination or the knowledge. They didn't realize what this all meant," said the colonel, waving his hand at the rows of crates.

"Let's start with the real estate. What were they after?"

"Let them tell you," said Greta curtly.

"Greta—I believe that is your name?"

"How brilliant of you to discover that."

"I intend to discover a great deal more tonight. I've many questions. I want honest answers. Is that clear?"

That amused her. She looked at the colonel and snorted. "Honest? He doesn't know what the word means."

He scowled and did not reply.

"I want honest answers from you, too."

"I'm not interested in telling you anything."

"This is not a law court. You will tell me exactly what I want to know," he said quietly.

"How do you expect to make me do that?" she said. "Put me on the Rack, or in the Iron Maiden?"

He knew what she was doing. Playing for time. The other two men could return at any moment. Doubtlessly, they were armed.

"The Iron Maiden? An interesting idea. Glad you mentioned it. I hadn't thought of it," he said calmly, visualizing the hollow metal torture instrument, the female form with the interior spikes. "You'd just fit in there."

She stared at him. Was he joking? Impossible to tell from his flat tones. Impossible to read anything on that masked face with the unseen eyes, a face like a stone statue. Then she changed her mood as effortlessly as the moon coming from behind a cloud. She smiled and her voice was soft and alluring.

"Please, who are you? How did you know about the witch and the masked stranger? Please, tell me about yourself."

"I am asking the questions," he said sharply, ignoring the invitation in her voice. "I want to get into those crates, but first, let's clear up this real-estate story."

She folded her arms on her chest and looked at him stubbornly. "I know nothing about that and care less," she said.

"I think you know everything that goes on here," he said.

She stared at him without replying. She appeared to be challenging him, to see what he would do.

"I want answers. We don't need the Iron Maiden. We have Devil."

At the sound of his name, Devil looked at his master who pointed toward the woman. The wolf walked slowly toward her. She stared at the pale-blue eyes and the long shining fangs, and shrank against a crate.

"What do you want to know?" she gasped.

Devil had that way with people. He was so big and shaggy he terrified them. Poor Devil, thought the Phantom. To be so misunderstood. He was trained to attack criminals and hold them. He would never use those sharp fangs on a human except in self-defense. Now, he sat before her, his long red tongue hanging over his open jaw, and panted softly.

"We're going to get into those crates, especially DV-1, but first let's clear up this real-estate buying. I don't believe your thugs are interested in farming. I don't think you and the colonel are. What's this all about?"

"Tell him, Hermann," she said, without taking her eyes off Devil.

"I have no interest in the matter. Let him ask Gerhart," he said stiffly.

"Gerhart is one of the two in the valley with the stubborn farmer?"

The colonel barely nodded.

"And the other one?"

"Wolfgang."

"When Gerhart and Wolfgang return, I will question them. You are here. You will tell me what you know."

"Believe me, I have neither knowledge nor interest in their stupid venture," he said loftily.

"Not true," said the Phantom calmly. "When your two thugs, Hans and the fat one, tried to force Roko to sell, you were waiting in the car for them."

The Phantom hadn't been able to make out the men in the car at that time, but it seemed like a good guess. It was. The colonel flushed.

"I waited, true. But I had no interest or knowledge."

"Devil," said the Phantom quietly, looking at the colonel. Devil walked slowly to the colonel and sat before him, his jaws open, his red tongue lolling out of his jaws.

"But it was all their idea. I don't know the details," cried the colonel, staring at the big wolf.

"Never mind the details. Just tell what you know."

"Ask her. She knows more," he said desperately, still reluctant to give in.

"Don't try to hide behind my skirts," said Greta, amused by the colonel's fear.

"Not a good place to hide," said the Phantom dryly, glancing at her scanty miniskirt.

"You noticed my legs," she said with a slight smile. "A good sign."

"Talk," said the Phantom to the colonel.

"I heard what you told him earlier. You wanted me as part of the deal," she went on. "We'll talk about that later." She smiled more broadly.

A tough-minded woman, he told himself, able to flirt with a gun pointing at her.

"Colonel, Hermann, no more delay. Talk."

Devil yawned. His wide-open jaws could almost engulf a man's head. The colonel looked down that throat and began to talk.

"I detailed Gerhart here three years ago for caretaker duties," he began. "He was the only one among us with scientific training."

"What kind of scientific training?"

"Geology."

"Go on."

"During his off-hours, he made several surveys of the area, using instruments and techniques with which I am not familiar since I have no interest in scientific matters, being more concerned with the humanities, music, literature, and—"

"Let's get back to Gerhart."

"As you wish," said the colonel, annoyed at the interruption. "Gerhart reported his findings to me. They were, of course, preliminary and required verification of a substantive nature which we were to receive later."

"May I sit down," said Greta, obviously bored with this

recital. The Phantom nodded. She sat on the edge of a low platform on which crates were stacked.

"But even with the verification, I refused to be a part of what I considered a foolhardy venture, even, one might say, a red herring. I refused to be diverted from my main purpose. I have followed that principle all my life, to choose a goal and stay with it."

"Oh, for God's sake, get on with it," muttered Greta. "But Gerhart and Wolfgang and Hans and the others were not to be denied. They smelled riches, they said, something they could understand, not like this," he said, waving his hand at the crates. "How could they be expected to understand what we have here. They're low-born ignorant-peasant types."

"Gerhart and Wolfgang are not low-born peasants," said Greta, rocking cross-legged on the platform.

"Perhaps not to you, considering your background," he said nastily.

"Thank you very much, Herr Count von--" she began in a mocking voice.

"No!" said the colonel sharply, shutting off her mention of his name.

The Phantom was listening patiently. The colonel was obviously trying to avoid coming to the point, again playing for time. But certain facts about these people were emerging from this rambling discourse. It was time now to get down to it.

"Okay," he said, using an Americanism he had picked up from his sweetheart, Diana Palmer. "What did Gerhart discover here in his scientific surveys?"

The colonel was about to answer, either vaguely, or to the point, when Devil suddenly perked up his ears and tensed, looking toward the dark office through the open doorway. There was a sound of footsteps, then voices.

"Where's the light?" said a heavy man's voice.

The colonel and Greta were alert, looking toward the doorway for Gerhart and Wolfgang. If they could only call out to them, warn them. The Phantom had moved at once to the wall alongside the open door. Greta opened her mouth, starting to speak.

"Shh," warned the Phantom. Devil was now in a low crouch on the floor.

"Colonel," called the same deep voice. "Colonel."

"Maybe they left," said another man's voice.

The Phantom pointed to Greta and the colonel.

"Guard," he said.

Devil turned silently to them, remaining in his low

crouch, his jaws open now, his great fangs glistening. The sudden change in the big animal was apparent to the man and woman. He was poised to attack if they moved. They felt that. They remained rigid.

"What's the matter with the light in here?" said the voice out of the dark office. That was the bulb in the ceiling fixture that the Phantom had smashed.

The Phantom pointed to the colonel and said softly, "Call."

"Hello," said the colonel in a cracked voice.

"Colonel, where are you?"

He looked at the Phantom who nodded. He licked his dry lips and said, "Here."

"Do you know the light in this office doesn't work?" said the voice, growing louder as the man approached the doorway.

"You should have seen that guy's face when I started to bite his neck," continued the voice with a laugh.

"How about his wife when I went for her? Man, was she something!" said the other voice deeper in the dark room. The first man reached the doorway at that point, and saw the colonel and Greta facing the crouching wolf, an unexpected sight in the pale light. He was a big husky man wearing the familiar broad hat and black cape. He was grinning.

"Hey, what—?" he started to say. An iron fist swung from the side. The impact was so hard that he blacked out before he could utter a sound.

"Wolfgang," cried the other voice from the dark office. He evidently saw his companion fall, and turned to run the other way. At the same time, he drew his gun.

"Hold," said the Phantom to Devil as he raced through the doorway, bent low so that he was only waist-high. He knew that coming out of the lighted chamber, he was a visible target in the doorway. The man in the dark room had time to get off one shot that missed the Phantom by a hair's breadth. Then he was knocked to the floor with a flying tackle.

He was a strong man and he managed to struggle to his feet. This attack in the dark by an unknown assailant was terrifying, and his fear increased his strength. But he was no match for this quick opponent. A hard blow in his stomach doubled him up and a second smash on the jaw ended the fight. The Phantom picked him up and hurled him through the doorway where he landed with a crash on top of the other man lying there.

The Phantom strode through the doorway, stepping over the two men. The colonel and Greta had remained in their places, held by a crouching Devil. They stared at the masked figure, stunned by this violence. They looked at the two big men on the floor, for whom they had delayed and procrastinated—their last hope. The Phantom stood before them and he seemed to loom gigantically in this pale light. His voice was deep and cold as though it came from a dark cave.

"Now, we will really talk," he said. And they both knew there was no more question about that. The time had come.

("The cold voice of the angry Phantom can freeze the blood," —old jungle saying.)

CHAPTER 20

The two men on the floor, Gerhart and Wolfgang, hadn't moved. Their heavy breathing filled the room.

"They've both got that thing on their faces, like Malo and that bartender," cried Greta.

The bluish mark, the Sign of the Skull, was clearly visible on the jaw of each man. "What is that thing?" Greta continued, an edge of hysteria in her voice.

The Phantom ignored her question. "I'm looking for rope, but I don't see any. That baling wire will have to do. Bring it to me." The colonel obeyed, getting the wire which was wrapped around a wooden frame.

"I've left your people spilled all over. Time to bring a little order here," the Phantom continued. There was a box of tools on the air conditioner. He rummaged in it until he found what he was looking for, a wire-cutter. The man and woman watched, fascinated. In his skintight costume, he was an incredible figure. And they had been hunting him?

He quickly bound the wrists and ankles of Gerhart and Wolfgang, then did a similar job on the first guard he'd met in this chamber. The man was just starting to stir. ("When the Phantom hits, they stay hit," —old sailor saying.) Then he turned on his flashlight and, at his order, Greta and the colonel entered the dark office. Two more men were lying there. At the Phantom's direction, they carried one after the other into the crate room, where the Phantom bound them with wire. Next were the two who had been on ladders outside the office. They lay where the Phantom had left them. Greta and the colonel carried them back, one at a time.

"This is not a woman's work," complained Greta, staggering under her share of the weight of these big men.

"What are you complaining about? You're barely helping," said the colonel, gasping for breath. He was hauling the main weight, carrying the men by the shoulders.

"Quite right, Greta," said the Phantom as he tied up the last two. "Not a woman's work at all. None of it. You might have thought of that before you came to Koqania."

Breathing hard from her efforts, she glared at him, and muttered obscenities under her breath.

Binding these men had been a necessary precaution. All would start to stir soon. It was best to have them under control before this happened.

"Now, your turn, Colonel. Turn around."

The colonel stood erect and indignant. "It is not necessary. You can trust me," he said.

"It is necessary. I cannot trust you," said the Phantom as he bound the colonel's wrists.

Greta stood up and extended her arms. "Me, too?" she said angrily.

"Not yet," said the Phantom.

"You trust me?" She smiled.

"No. But if it is necessary, I will do it." He bent over Gerhart and Wolfgang. "I didn't mean to hit them so hard. They'll be out for a while. Colonel, let's get down to it. You tell me what they are looking for."

The colonel cleared his throat and began in a pompous manner. "Despite lack of definitive and substantive verification, but going upon fairly conclusive preliminary—"

"Colonel," said the Phantom sharply, "say it in one word."

"Oil," said the colonel.

Oil. It was as though a fog had suddenly lifted and the little town and valley tucked between mountain ranges were clearly visible once more.

"Tell it to me simply," said the Phantom.

"As I said, I sent Gerhart here on a caretaker assignment."

"Caretaker for this?" asked the Phantom, glancing at the crates.

The colonel nodded. "Gerhart had been a geologist. He

worked for many large companies in Africa and the Middle east. Something about this terrain gave him the idea that oil existed in this area."

Now that the need to delay was over, the colonel spoke clearly and quickly in a precise manner that fit his military posture.

"I don't know how he came to this conclusion. You'll have to ask him."

"They use sonar and radar and that sort of thing," said Greta, tired of only listening.

"Have there been oil wells drilled in this area?" said the Phantom.

"No, that's what got Gerhart so excited. Virgin territory," said the colonel. "A term you'd have difficulty understanding," he added dryly to Greta.

She shook her head as if at a poor joke. "You really are a complete ass," she said.

"Go on," said the Phantom.

"It was their plan to buy the entire valley for as little as possible."

"They?"

"All of them—Gerhart, Wolfgang, Hans, Malo, Gunda the tavern owner, the others."

"They all went wild over the idea of oil, all of them including him," said Greta scornfully.

"I beg your pardon," said Hermann stiffly.

"You pretended to be above it all, but I noticed when it came to deciding on shares, how to cut the pie, you got your part of it," said Greta.

"How about you?" snapped the colonel. "You demanded to cut in, too, or you wouldn't play witch."

She shrugged. "Why not? Whatever the play was, I wanted to be in it. I gave up plenty for this operation."

The colonel laughed scornfully. "You gave up what? A tenth-rate career going nowhere?"

That stung her more than anything that had been said. "Tenth-rate?" she blazed, jumping to her feet. "Did you read what they said about me in Cologne and Dusseldorf?"

"Wait, let's take it back," said the Phantom. "You all apportioned shares among yourselves. Shares of what?"

"Shares of hope that there might be oil," said Greta.

"It's absurd," said the colonel bitterly. "Here we sit on one hundred million dollars, and we argue about a few stinking oil wells that don't even exist."

"One hundred million?" said the Phantom, glancing at the

crates.

"At least. Maybe two hundred million," said Greta.

"We'll get to the crates in a moment," said the Phantom. "If the stuff in them is that valuable, why worry about developing an oil field that might not even exist?"

"Because they are lummoxes. I told you. They don't have the breeding, the imagination, or the brains to know what we have here," said the colonel. "Ignorant, low-born peasants."

"So that's what you think, Herr Count," said a rumbling voice. It was Gerhart. Lying on the floor, hands and wrists bound, his eyes were open. He strained at his bonds and struggled to a sitting position to see what held him. He shook his arms and legs angrily. The wire held. Then he saw the Phantom and his eyes widened.

"Who the hell are you?" he said. "Greta, who is he?"

"The mysterious stranger called the Phantom," said Greta. "You see, I told you all about that. You thought it was—what did you call it—a fairy tale."

Gerhart's thick lips hung loosely, his mouth open. "You mean with the old witch and all that?" he said.

She nodded.

"But it wasn't real. We know it was just an old story," he said slowly, staring as though seeing a ghost.

"Ask him," said Greta.

Gerhart looked about and saw Wolfgang lying near him. "Where are all the others?"

"There are no more others," said the colonel.

"Dead?"

"Some. Some like you."

"How? Who did this?"

The colonel glanced at the Phantom. Gerhart's mouth still hung open.

"You think there's oil in this valley?" said the Phantom.

Gerhart reacted in surprise and glared at Greta and the colonel.

"You told him our secret?" he shouted.

"When he's got a gun pointed at you, what do you do?" said Greta.

"Exactly. What did all those farmers do when you threatened to kill them, or scared them half to death unless they gave you their land?"

"Gave? We buy," snarled Gerhart.

"Buy. With what you give them, you steal the land. You steal, and if you can't, you kill."

"No proof of that," said the colonel sharply.

"Raimond, Piotr, how many others?" said the Phantom.

"We know nothing about them," said the colonel.

"Nothing," said Gerhart, suddenly a witness on trial.

"That's for the courts to decide," said the Phantom. "Back to the oil. When you couldn't buy the land for next to nothing, you used terror. Where did you get the idea of vampires?"

Greta gestured at the colonel. "His bright thought."

"Actually, it was Malo. He spent years here. He knew all about this place. He told us. We couldn't believe it. We talked to the ignorant peasants in the valley. Amazingly, they did believe in it. They do believe it still. The vampires and the witch." In spite of the wires on his wrists, he laughed. "Understandable. They're Slav, you know, a word akin to slave."

"My mother was bom here," said Greta sharply.

Now Wolfgang muttered and coughed and opened his eyes. When he discovered the wires on his wrists and ankles, he went through the same contortions that Gerhart had tried. To no avail. The wires held. Struggling made them cut into the flesh, so one didn't struggle long.

"How much land have you stolen so far in this valley?" asked the Phantom.

"Wolfgang's the statistician," said the colonel.

The Phantom loomed over the newly awakened man. Devil walked over and stuck his long muzzle into the startled man's face.

"You heard my question. How much?"

"How much what?" cried Wolfgang, certain his last moment had come.

"How much land have you stolen in Koqania Valley?"

"I don't know."

Devil prodded him in the neck with his cold nose. Then lapped his cheek with the long tongue.

"About half," he cried.

The other three men bound by the Phantom were regaining consciousness, moaning and muttering. When their eyes could focus properly, they stared at the masked man and the wolf.

"Remember the man in the tavern I told you about, the one who beat up Gunda?" said the colonel to Greta. She nodded. "This is the one."

"How do you know?"

"Those marks on the jaw. Gunda had one. So did Malo."

They were suddenly silent. Gunda, the tavernkeeper. The Phantom could almost hear their thoughts. Two of their number were still at large. Gunda, the tavernkeeper, and the other one he'd left in the torture chamber. The colonel and Greta exchanged glances. Those two, Gunda and the other one, might come at any time. They were armed. All hope was not lost. Both showed sudden renewed arrogance.

"I believe I've heard enough of the land and oil story. A lot more detail is to come out, but the courts can handle that. Now, let's talk about the crates," said the Phantom.

The colonel and Greta remained unresponsive.

"Maybe they're tired of talking. Gerhart, what about the crates?"

"He doesn't have to know any more," said the colonel quickly.

"I don't know nothing about that stuff," said Gerhart. "If you ask me, it's a lot of junk."

"Gerhart!" said the colonel angrily.

"Junk," repeated Gerhart. "Waste of time. If I told you once, I told you a thousand times we're going to make it in oil."

"Forget the oil. Get to the crater," said the Phantom.

The colonel and Greta glanced at each other. Gunda might come.

The Phantom took the crate from beside the air conditioner.

"DV-1," he read on the side of the crate. "I've waited a long time to see what this is."

"No, not yet," said the colonel.

"Wait," said Greta hurriedly. "That crate's not important. There's a lot more you should know about us."

"Not important? You all gave me the impression it was worth a fortune," said the Phantom.

"Just a ploy to keep you from the real valuables," said the colonel slyly. And he exchanged shrewd glances with Greta and the men on the floor.

"Give me the screwdriver. I want to get this open now," said the Phantom.

"Believe me, a waste of time. Nothing in it, really," said the colonel.

"He's right," said Greta. "The real things are stored down the hall. Gerhart, what did you say about all these crates?"

"Junk," said Gerhart, the Neanderthal.

"Junk," said Greta.

"Junk," echoed the colonel.

"By the way," said the Phantom, as he began to loosen the first screw, "if you're waiting for Gunda and that other man, don't hold your breath until they come. I left them unconscious in that delightful torture chamber. Chief Peta was also with them. By now, they're safely behind bars in his jail."

They stared at each other, Greta at the colonel, at Wolfgang and Gerhart, their sudden arrogance deflating like a punctured inner tube, then at the Phantom as he worked on the crate.

"Be careful with that," screamed the colonel, his voice turning almost falsetto. "It's priceless!"

CHAPTER 21

A s everyone in the chamber watched tensely, he unpacked the crate. Inside the wooden box was a thick layer of styrofoam, a soft porous insulating material. Beneath that a cover of fine white linen. He carefully lifted the cloth and its contents from the crate, then unwrapped it. It had an elaborately carved gold frame. It was a painting, the portrait of a proud young man with long black hair, wearing a rich green-velvet jacket. Around his neck was a heavy glittering necklace of gold and jewels. The Phantom looked at it for a long moment. There was perfection about this painting, like a rare jewel.

"Is it damaged at all?" asked the colonel in a strained voice. The Phantom faced the painting toward him so he could see it. The colonel stared at it.

"Not a scratch. Perfect!" he said excitedly.

The Phantom had no great knowledge of art, but through the years he'd had an occasional opportunity to visit the great museums of the world—the Louvre in Paris, the Pitti and Uffizi palaces in Florence, the Metropolitan in New York among others. He had never seen this painting, but he knew something about it. It was one of the most famous portraits on earth, and it had been lost for over thirty years. It was Leonardo da Vinci's *Portrait of Lorenzo di Medici as a Young Man*. To call it priceless was probably not overstating it. Every painting has a price, however fabulous, if it is put up for sale. It is doubtful that the Dutch Museum from which it had been "requisitioned" would ever have sold it, any more than the Louvre would be apt to sell a sister masterpiece. *The Mona Lisa.* Da Vinci . . . DV-1.

"I suppose there is no question that it's genuine," said the Phantom. The colonel shook with anger.

"It's authenticity is beyond doubt. We have the papers for it, all the way back to William of Orange, that purchase being made for him in Rome by none other than Peter Paul Rubens," said the colonel, as though auctioning it off.

The Phantom walked among the racks holding the crates. He chose three more and brought them back beneath the pale overhead light.

"No time to look at them all now, but I did notice these and I want to have a look at them. MA-1, R-2, and FH- 4."

Each painting was similarly crated in styrofoam and linen, and all appeared to be in perfect condition.

MA-1 was a striking oil of a regal old man in flowing robes reaching out to touch the forefinger of a languorous, beautiful nude young man. Any of the millions of pilgrims and tourists who have visited the Sistine Chapel in the Vatican and strained their necks and eyes to stare at the mighty ceiling would recognize this as *The Creation of Adam by the Hand of God.* Among those millions had been the Phantom.

"I never knew Michelangelo did a small painting of that scene," he said.

"Not many did. He painted it especially for the bedroom of Pope Julian. It later passed into the hands of the Hapsburg emperors, where it remained until we—" the colonel stumbled on the word and stopped guiltily, having said too much.

"I want to know more about 'we' in a moment," said the Phantom. "After I have opened these other two."

One of the "other two" was R-2. It was immediately recognizable. One of that long series of self-portraits by Rembrandt. Unlike the later self-portraits, marked by age and sadness, this was a happy, bright young face.

"One of his earliest, said to be his personal favorite for he never sold it in his lifetime, even in his most difficult times," said the colonel, sounding like a museum guide. FH-4 was a ruddy, mischievous girl by the Dutch master Franz Hals. The Phantom looked over the rows of crates. If the paintings were all of this quality, one hundred million dollars was not an exaggeration.

"Are they all like this?"

"You picked several of the choice items, but there are others equal and almost equal," said the colonel tensely. "This masked man, this hijacker, is going to loot our treasures and there's nothing, nothing we can do," he finished almost in tears.

"Is that why you came here?" asked Greta. The Phantom did not reply.

"Why else?" asked the colonel shrilly. "What else would he do?"

"I know what else he can do," said Greta. "He can kill all of us. And who would know?"

The chamber was deathly still as the men stared at the masked figure.

"Is that what you expect?" he said.

"I've learned to face facts," she said flatly.

"If you were in my place, it's what you would do," he said.

She lowered her head. "Don't listen to her. She's crazy," said the colonel. "You said you wanted a deal? You said you wanted Greta. Take her and half the paintings."

"You swine," shouted Greta. She leaped to her feet and rushed at the colonel, her long red nails aimed at his face. He was helpless to defend himself. The Phantom reached her first and pulled her back. She leaned against him, and surprisingly, began to weep softly.

"Did you hear that swine? He's ready to sell me, anything to save his filthy hide," she sobbed.

"Don't be taken in by her. She can cry at the drop of a hat. She does her best acting offstage," said the colonel viciously. She turned to go at him again with her sharp nails, but the Phantom held her arm.

"Sit down there. I don't have time for all this." She sat, staring at him with wide tear-filled eyes. The tears ran down her cheeks, smudging her mascara.

"Colonel, where did all this come from?"

The colonel sighed. "It's a long story."

"Then make it short."

"It is difficult. Where shall I start?"

"At the beginning. Start with your real name."

"I am Count Hermann Adolphus von der Kotthausen, colonel retired of the Imperial German Army," he began proudly. "My uncle was General Karl Maximus von der—"

"It's not necessary to discuss your uncle" said the Phantom.

"As you will see, it is most necessary," replied the colonel. "He was Deputy Commander under Field Marshal Hermann

Goering, a name you may know." The Phantom nodded.

"As the Imperial German Army crumbled under the ignorant criminal failures of the Nazi trash . . ." He paused and glared at Gerhart and Wolfgang, both of whom growled. He was obviously mentioning old enmities that existed between them. "Where was I?" he said.

"When the German army crumbled," said Greta with a harsh laugh.

"Yes, let me go back slightly."

"Not too far. Time is short," warned the Phantom.

"It is necessary. As the world knows, the Field Marshal was an inveterate collector of art. Collector is a polite word for thief."

Once again, Gerhart and Wolfgang growled, but he ignored them. "It is fully documented that as the Imperial armies conquered the Low Countries and invaded France, the agents of the field marshal swept the museums clean, taking whatever the inhabitants had been unable to hide first. Even hidden treasures were found, often by torture, all for the edification of the great fat parvenu beast, Goering."

The Phantom was amazed by the self-righteous tone of the man who only a few hours earlier was presiding over the torture on the Rack of the police chief. And who had presided over murder as well. But he said nothing.

"This collection was divided into several parts, and as the war turned against us, due to the criminal negligence of the Nazi trash. . ." Gerhart struggled with the wires at his wrist, but only succeeded into digging them into his flesh. Apparently, Gerhart had been part of this "trash."

"As the war turned against us," continued the colonel, pleased with the reaction he aroused in the helpless Gerhart, "it was decided to conceal the objects in various hideaways. My uncle. General Karl Maximus von der Kotthausen, was in charge of this operation."

"Where were you at the time?"

"I was a very young junior officer on the staff of my uncle," said the colonel.

"Were you ever very young?" asked Greta spitefully.

"I wasn't even shaving yet," snapped the colonel. "Now, during an earlier period of the war, when we were winning, when the Imperial General Staff was still running things"—he glanced at the angry Gerhart, still seated on the floor—"my uncle commanded an occupation force for a time here in Koqania. Several times, during quiet days, we explored these ruins and the endless cellars. So when the time came to conceal the plundered treasures, this was a natural place to think of—one of several.

But my uncle chose the best items for this place. His technicians installed the equipment here, the air conditioning, the power and other utilities, living quarters, and whatnot. Then these treasures, expertly packed, were brought in. The place was sealed off by our forces, so that no one in the valley knew what we did.

"When the war ended, my uncle realized it would be difficult to maintain secrecy without armed forces. We had both been amused by the medieval superstitions connected to the castle, the tales of vampires and witches, goblins and other supernatural monstrosities. I'd like to take credit for the idea, but I must admit it came from a fellow junior officer, a young poet who was killed later at Stalingrad, that most colossal of catastrophes engineered by the Nazis."

At this point, Gerhart and Wolfgang could only glare at him silently, having worn out all their fury.

"But Joachim, that was his name, came up with the idea at a staff meeting. Vampires. The tradition already existed and was still strong among these peasants. Why not take advantage of it? We did. While our forces were still here, some of us disguised ourselves as we thought vampires might look, and roamed the fields at night."

"And occasionally slashed a throat?" asked the Phantom.

The colonel nodded. "Yes, that was done now and then under the orders of my uncle, the general. How could vampires be believed unless they acted like vampires? The plan worked. The ruins here were said to be the home of the vampires. In truth, this was a perfect place, with actual torture chambers. They were here when we arrived. We put some of the devices to use now and then, letting the 'victim' escape to spread the word.

"After the war, I remained in hiding with my uncle. The crowd at Nuremberg were searching for him to add to that obscene circus they called the war crimes trials."

"Did they find him?" asked the Phantom.

Greta laughed at that. "Tell him where they found your precious uncle," she said.

"He had an accident. He fell down a flight of stairs."

"He was drunk. The stairs led to the local house of ill repute, your high-born art-expert uncle's favorite spot," said Greta spitefully.

"You shut up, you foul-mouthed slut!" shouted the colonel, suddenly furious. She had touched a raw nerve. His adoration of his late uncle, the general, was obvious.

"Before that awful day," he went on, "we discussed this place often, my uncle and I. For, if the truth were known, this was his hideout. A few of us came here from time to time, members of his staff, deserters from his regiments. Never more than a dozen. But we kept the treasures intact, and we kept the vampire tradition alive."

"The fools stayed on here for years," said Greta.

"Only until the war trials were forgotten, until we were no longer hunted like criminals."

"Naturally, you never returned any of the stolen art."

"I prefer to think of it all as mine, ours, legally by right of conquest," said the colonel stiffly. "Think what Napoleon brought back from Egypt and Italy. France is full of those treasures."

"Your logic is curious. You just called Field Marshal Goering a thief for doing the same thing, an opinion I would agree with. However, let's get on. Have you sold much of it?"

Greta and the men laughed at that, bitter laughter.

"How can we sell? These are famous works, known in every country. Major buyers would be afraid. Oh, we sold a few minor works to keep the pot boiling as they say. Nothing big," said the colonel.

This was ironic. These conspirators had sat on this vast treasure for over a generation, fearing to dispose of it because of possible exposure. It reminded the Phantom of Croesus in the old myth—everything he touched turned to gold, but there was nothing he could eat or drink.

"There was that big dealer from Brazil," said Gerhart in his rasping voice. The others looked at him quickly in annoyance. He smiled guiltily and looked away.

"What big dealer from Brazil?" asked the Phantom.

"A gallery owner, one of the few we ever brought here. Offered a half million for the lot—a half million!" said the colonel indignantly.

"That was a lot of money. We should have taken it," growled Gerhart.

"Half a million, you thick-headed peasant," shouted the colonel. "For these treasures worth a hundred, two hundred million?"

"What happened to the dealer from Brazil?" asked the Phantom.

"A good question," said Greta, grinning like a naughty child.

"Guess he went back to Brazil," said the colonel.

Greta laughed. The Phantom looked around the chamber. The men stared at him coldly.

"Did he threaten to expose you unless you accepted his offer, or were you merely afraid he might talk?"

No answer. Gerhart yawned, the colonel looked at his

shoes.

"Where did you bury him?" asked the Phantom.

No answer. The men looked at Greta as if daring her to talk. She started to speak, then stopped.

"A dealer from Brazil. He probably was ready to make a cash offer of some kind. You'd hardly take checks down here, or credit cards. I doubt that you buried that cash with him," said the Phantom. Again, a stony silence.

"How many other rich dealers or collectors came here through the years and never left these ruins? I begin to get the picture now," said the Phantom. "Do you know why I picked DV-1, R-2, FH-4, and MA-1 to open? Because they were the only ones I saw that weren't tied with wire and would be easier to open. Why these?"

The colonel shrugged. "You have such marvelous powers of deduction, Mr. Mystery Man. Perhaps you can tell us."

"Perhaps I can guess. Because those are the treasures you showed the prospective buyers. They would excite any art dealer."

"If we are such cold-blooded killers as you would have us, why go to so much trouble?" said the colonel. "Why not just get them here and knock them over the head?"

"I doubt if such dealers or collectors would come here with large amounts of cash to buy sight unseen, not to these ruins with obvious crooks."

The men reacted angrily to that; Greta laughed.

"But after seeing these four masterpieces, a deal could be made. They would come back with their cash—one thousand, twenty thousand, fifty thousand—to obtain treasures worth millions. And I would guess those buyers and their cash never left these ruins," said the Phantom.

"And when these mythical rich buyers disappeared, would no one ever think to come and search for them?" said the colonel.

"I'm certain you took care of that ahead of time. The buyers would never be told this location. They would be brought here at night, blindfolded or in a closed car, so they never could relocate the castle."

The colonel looked at the others and shrugged.

"A neat theory. There are no witnesses, no proof," he said.

"I'm certain the proof is buried not far from where we are standing in unmarked graves. There will be time to find them," said the Phantom.

"I don't know why you waste time with all of this," said the colonel. "You try to speak as though you are a policeman. What we see is a masked man, a hijacker come to rob us. Whoever you are, you cannot dispose of these treasures any easier than we could, less so perhaps. At least, through the years we have made the proper connections. We can still find buyers."

"To lure here and rob and murder," said the Phantom.

"If you wish to join forces with us, it may be possible. Alone, you gain nothing. With us, you share all we get, however we get it. As for Greta, if you want her," the colonel said, shrugging, "That will be a private matter between you. For my part, you are welcome to her."

"Thanks a lot," said Greta.

"Greta, I need one more clue to solve the puzzle. You are it," said the Phantom.

"I beg your pardon," said Greta, smiling softly at him.

"How did you get to be the witch?"

CHAPTER 22

"My father was a German soldier, like all these pigs," said Greta. Gerhart and Wolfgang laughed. The colonel was insulted.

"Don't compare me to a common soldier of the ranks!" he snapped. She bowed her head in mock apology.

"Forgive me Herr Colonel Count von der Kotthausen."

"But your mother was from Koqania," said the Phantom.

"How did you know that?" she said, startled.

"You mentioned it before."

"Do you remember everything I said?" she said coyly.

"Yes. Please go on."

"From the beginning?"

"If you like."

"There's nothing important about the early part," she said bitterly. "My father was killed in the war, at Stalingrad, I think. I was an infant in my mother's arms. We were sent from one refugee camp to another. I spent my childhood in them. Horrible places. In my teens, I finally escaped to the streets of Berlin."

"And she stayed in the streets from then on," said the colonel, unable to resist the dig. She glared at him but did not reply.

The Phantom was surprised. The early period she was talking about was the closing years of World War II, over thirty years ago. He hadn't thought her that old. He had seen her only by candlelight and this pale chamber light. He turned on his flashlight, shining it briefly in her face. She shielded her eyes.

"Is that necessary?" she snapped.

"Sorry. Go on."

She was not in her early twenties as he had thought. Despite clever makeup, there were tiny lines making her a decade older. The colonel and his hoodlums all had to be older than they looked. Perhaps there had been plastic surgery, not for vanity but for disguise.

"I did various things to support myself," she continued. The colonel snorted at that. "Then I became an actress, an entertainer. I sang, I worked in provincial companies. I was quite good. Everyone said so. Film companies were interested. I could have been a star, an international star."

"Another Marlene," said the colonel.

"You liked me well enough, especially in *Hamsel and Gretel*," she snapped.

"Hansel and Gretel?"

Greta laughed. "That's where it all started, when he saw me in the play."

"You played Gretel?" asked the Phantom.

"No. I played the witch." She laughed. "The same costume I was wearing when you first met me," she said grinning. "The colonel was too cheap to buy me a new one."

"And he convinced you to come back here and play the witch?"

"That came later and it was my idea, not his. He never had an idea of his own in his life," she said.

The colonel bristled, but said nothing.

"I'd heard about the witch of Hunda from my mother when I was a child. She believed there really was a witch. And she told me about the mysterious stranger, called the Phantom, who had chained the witch—a masked man as tall as an oak. That was part of the story, too," she continued, looking at the Phantom with wide eyes. "And when we got reports there was a masked man seen in the woods, and when you came into the ruins and we saw, I could hardly believe it. Who are you really?" she said, and for the moment, she was the wide-eyed child of long ago.

"Never mind that. He brought you here to play the witch. Why? They had the vampires. Why did they need the witch?"

"Added insurance against intruders. It also amused us," said the colonel. "We learned an interesting thing. These ignorant peasants around here were afraid of vampires, but even the idea of the witch terrified them."

"They thought she could hear them wherever they were," said

Greta. "They blamed all their bad luck on the witch. When a cow died, or a horse broke its leg, the witch did it."

"It was, you might say, in their folklore," said the colonel pompously.

"In spite of warnings from their parents, children sometimes came here to play. We let them see the witch," said Greta. "So the word would get back."

"What about the two you tried to kidnap from the church?"

"That was different. They saw me changing into my costume. We weren't too sure how much they saw, or would tell."

"So you decided to kill them?"

"Kill the children? Oh, no," said the colonel, as if horrified by the idea. "Merely to question them."

"On the Rack, or in the Iron Maiden?"

The men remained silent.

"What about the young farmer called Raimond?"

Greta smiled wickedly and glanced at the colonel. "Ask him."

"On sunny days, she had the habit of swimming in that pool by the moat—*au naturel*, you might say," said the colonel stiffly. "That fool Raimond had, for some reason best known to him, taken to watching these ruins through an old telescope. That day, he saw her swimming."

"And reported it?" said the Phantom.

"Reported nothing. He came charging over, hoping to find what he had seen."

"Greta, as you say, *au naturel*?"

"Exactly. She saw him coming. Instead of hiding, she waited for him."

"I put on my robe," she said irritably.

"Yes, and there she sat on a rock, chatting with this boob, ready to ruin everything," said the colonel.

"I told you, I told him nothing," said Greta wearily. "He thought I was a tourist."

"She arranged to meet the idiot on the road that night. On the road!" said the colonel scornfully.

"He wasn't an idiot. He was young and handsome. I was bored with this place. Bored with you, all of you," she shouted. The men looked at her coldly.

"It could have ruined everything," said the colonel.

"Did you meet him on the road?" asked the Phantom.

She shook her head and lowered it. "They got there first," she said in a dull voice.

"There is no evidence of that, no proof," said the colonel quickly.

"Let's go back," said the Phantom slowly. He had known

many evil people and sordid crimes in the past, but this recital was beginning to sicken him.

"The colonel saw you play the witch and brought you here?"

"He persuaded me. At first I thought it was foolish, hut he promised me everything, even a castle on the Rhine, jewels, everything I wanted—millions."

"You also became his girl?"

"That went with it for a while," she said shortly.

"I gather your duties were not limited to playing the old witch?" said the Phantom.

"Meaning what?"

"Buyers were lured here by various means. I'm guessing, of course. Isn't it possible these men used you as bait to attract their big fish?"

"Yes, there was a good deal of that. I even flew to Brazil to make sure that one took the bait," she said.

"Greta!" said the colonel sharply.

"I think I've heard enough. Come, Greta."

The men stared at him. Greta's face brightened.

"You're taking me with you?" she asked eagerly.

"Yes."

"And you're taking those paintings. Is that your cut?" said the colonel anxiously.

"Yes, I'll take those, since they're open."

"What about us? You can't leave us tied up like this," said Gerhart.

Greta grasped the Phantom's arm. Her voice and eyes were soft as she looked at him, and she pressed against him as she spoke.

"Listen to me. We don't need them. They didn't know what to do with this stuff. I do. There are places. The Middle East, for one. Full of nothing but money. They'll buy and ask no questions, believe me," she said intensely.

"And them?"

Greta looked about the chamber slowly, at Gerhart and Wolfgang, at the other five of the gang who were awake now, and finally at the colonel.

"Kill them," she said quietly.

There was a sharp intake of breath from the men, all together like a chorus.

"Just like that?" said the Phantom.

"Of course. What choice have you? They'll never let you get away with all this and me. They'll come after us for as long as we live. You must see that," she said quickly.

"None of you understand," said the Phantom. "I'm taking Greta and these four paintings with me to Chief Ivor Peta at the stationhouse. The chief and his deputies will be back shortly to pick you all up."

The men stared. Then the colonel laughed, a short bitter laugh. Greta's eyes blazed. She screamed, then struck at the Phantom with her tiny fists, shrieking a string of obscenities. He grabbed her wrists in his powerful hand as Devil walked over to him, watching protectively.

"You will all have your day in court," he said.

"There were no witnesses, no proof," shouted Colonel Count Hermann Adolphus von der Kotthausen.

The Phantom released Greta and started toward the men. She turned and ran out of the room. The Phantom snapped his fingers and pointed. Devil bounded out after her. A moment later, her scream was heard as she was stopped and pulled back harmlessly to the doorway by the big gray wolf.

"You wanted him to kill us," said the colonel grimly. "I hope they hang you, you little beast!"

The Phantom busied himself for a few moments, binding each man securely, to a separate rack with bailing wire.

"You may all get hung," he said as he took Greta's arm. "There is trial by jury in this little place. But everyone in Koqania is related—jury, judges, lawyers—as you know, Greta. They'll all be highly interested to know what happened here through the years to their relatives and friends, as well as to those rich foreign visitors."

CHAPTER 23

The revelations at the ruins of Koqania created an international sensation. Through the news media, the world had heard the earlier reports of the plague of vampires and the witch. Now that the amazing truth was coming out, interest everywhere was enormous. Reporters and camera crews from every major country sped to tiny Koqania. Tourists flooded the place. Normally the little town of Koqania could only accommodate a score of visitors. The thousands who poured in were put up in private homes, on farms, in tents. The rickety railroad arranged a special daily round-trip excursion for one-day visitors. The ruins were cordoned off and guarded by the local equivalent of a National Guard under the leadership of Chief Ivor Peta. Accredited press representatives were admitted to limited areas, and guided tours were permitted twice a day.

The visitors were fascinated by the torture chamber and by the chamber where the paintings had been stored. They had all been removed by that time. (An easier access had been found to that area—easier than the route traveled by the Phantom and Devil.) A special Art Council had been appointed by the United Nations to catalogue the stolen treasures and return them to their owners. This took several years to complete and almost started two minor wars among rival claimants.

The amazing story of the art treasures and the thirty-year vigil of the "vampires" and later the "witch" who guarded them was revealed gradually in the long trial. The main focus of attention was there. The tiny courtroom in Koqania could not hold a tenth of the visiting press, officials, and celebrities. So the trial was moved to the only building large enough in Koqania, a huge drafty wooden building used for the annual horse fair. There was an attempt to clean and deodorize the place before the trial. This was only partially successful, and the aroma of horse manure remained during the entire proceedings.

Gradually, the whole story was pieced together. And as the defendants confessed bits and pieces, old graves were found. Many international mysteries of missing persons were solved. A well-known art dealer from Sao Paulo, Brazil; the Emir of a prominent oil-rich sheikdom; a Japanese tycoon; a German dealer from Cologne; an American gangster; and a half-dozen others. Still others were somewhere in the vast ruins, but they were never found.

The trial proceeded slowly. Because of the prominence of many of the victims, the finest legal talent of four continents rushed to the spot. But the local lawyers needed little advice. Their relatives were among the almost countless victims of this thirty-year plot

Running like a thread through the entire trial was the mention now and then of the mysterious stranger, the masked man. It seemed this unknown person "had first blown the whistle on the entire deal" as an American journalist put it. But no one, including Chief Peta, or Roko the farmer, or the widow and children of dead Piotr, or the old cabdriver, or even the Lord Mayor himself, could tell much about him. The latter, pompous and officious during the entire trial, tried to impress everyone with his knowledge of the mysterious stranger, but finally had to admit he'd been in the dark the whole time.

To everyone's satisfaction, except the defendants, the trial came to a close. There were no higher courts of appeal in Koqania. This was it. Those sentenced to death by hanging for twelve premeditated murders, "most vicious and cruel," (twelve was all that could be proven) were Colonel Count Hermann Adolphus von der Kotthausen, Gerhart, Wolfgang, and a fourth man named Klotz. The colonel's part in all this was sensational. His uncle, the general, was well remembered and loathed as the wartime occupation ruler of Koqania. The other ten conspirators, including the woman, received life sentences.

Greta, the beautiful "witch," was a center of attraction throughout the trial. She was dazzling in her miniskirts, hotpants, sequin gowns, and furs. She was photographed a million times and her smiling face became as familiar as that of a film star. Even after her true identity was revealed, the Koqanians avoided her eyes, and, as many foreigners noted, treated her with some awe and fear. The legend of the witch of Hanta was deeply ingrained in these people, even the most educated, and it was hard to shake it off. When she was sentenced, she cried shrilly and shouted an amazing string of obscenities. The Koqanians present averted their eyes and put their hands over their ears to avoid the curse of this evil woman who (some believed) really was the witch.

Before the trial, shortly after the colonel and his men were hauled off to jail, the Phantom remained for a short time alone in the ruins with Devil. Using a flashlight, he retraced that long underground route that he and Devil had traveled in the dark. He stooped and he crawled as he had before. But now he could see the way. He paused to examine the ancient wall carvings. They were of people and animals. Some seemed to recount events, hunts, or battles, and seemed similar to such wall decorations in the Egyptian temples and pyramids. Others had a medieval look, knights in armor, battles with lances. Some were sensual, showing scenes of love. Here and there were mural paintings of animals, similar to ancient cave paintings. Archeologists were to have a field day in this place, and would find level upon level, subcellar beneath cellar, on and on, rivaling the seven levels of Troy.

He paused briefly at the torture chamber, and in a sudden fit of anger, rare for him, destroyed the ancient instrument called the Rack. He did this by tearing it from its metal moorings and smashing it repeatedly against the wall until it was a twisted mass of metal and kindling. No one would ever again be stretched on that horrible device. The rest would remain, when this chamber became a museum.

He made one more stop at the small cell that had served as a hideout for the Phantom through the generations. Here the eighth Phantom had been imprisoned by the real witch of Hanta. Here she had wept and pleaded with him—"I love you. I need you. I need you," she said, her perfume wafted through the bars. Now, almost three hundred years later, the descendant of that man, thirteen times removed, sat in this cell, trying to visualize the scene—the tearful face framed by shining golden hair in that narrow barred opening. The face he saw was Greta as the young witch, and he shook himself. No, not like that. But Greta's mother was of Koqania. By some miracle, could she be descended from that long-dead beauty? It was a tremendous thought, but the odds against it were too high. Yet, anything was possible. He dismissed that idea and sniffed the air. Was any of that ancient fragrance, the perfume of the witch, still there? Devil looked at him and sniffed also. Nothing.

In his previous two visits to this place, always brief and on the run, he had never had time to examine it. He did that now. There was light from the outside air shaft. The room was almost bare, beyond the little cot, table, and chair. He examined the walls carefully. He wanted to see if any of his ancestors from the eighth Phantom on, and that would mean twelve more generations, had written anything here, left any messages. He was disappointed to find there were none. Evidently, the Phantom did not write on walls. But as he searched behind the cot, pulling it away from the wall for that purpose, he found a loose stone. Intrigued, he pried it out of the wall and shone his flashlight beam into the dark hole. There was something in there. A roll of what appeared to be paper, but proved to be vellum, parchment.

It was bound with fine gold wire. He hurriedly unrolled it, and as he read the first lines by the light of his flashlight, he almost dropped both parchment and flashlight in surprise. It was the missing page, the final page from the Chronicle of the Eighth Phantom about the witch of Hanta.

He lit the candle on the little table at the side of the cot, and sitting there, read it by candlelight.

He recalled the last lines of this chronicle that he had read in the Skull Cave. Something about fire and towers crashing after the explosion of the castle, demons rushing about in the smoke, then the line that remained etched in his memory—"Then with the blonde witch of Hanta in my arms, I leaped from the wall to the moat far below."

That had been as far as the story went. The following page had been torn out. This was it. Fascinated, he read it aloud, as if to make sure he missed nothing. Devil sat on the floor of the cell, listening patiently.

"I will be brief now, and recount what followed and was most amazing. We survived the plunge and made our way down the slope to find shelter in a cave. For as the castle toppled and great sheets of flame lit the heavens, these heavens opened and a torrent of rain, thunder, and lightning assailed it. It was as if the very gods of this place were furious. The witch and I (perhaps by now, she reminds me, I should use her proper name, Heloise) stayed in this cave three days and nights until the storm abated.

In this time, let me confess, my world turned upside-down—if I may use such an expression—and I fell deeply in love with this wondrous woman, Heloise of Hanta, whom I had foolishly, stupidly, and clumsily believed to be a witch. She asks (watching me as I write this) that I add the adverb 'childishly.' So be it. I who had sought the love of a good woman over five continents and the seven seas, found it in this wind-swept cave in Koqania. One might ask, what did we eat during those three days? I will answer. There was fresh water in this cave, but for food there was love, and it sufficed.

"Now when the storm was over, the castle and the land about lay in waste and ruins. We hurriedly left that dismal place, and after a wondrous voyage made of minor adventure and major love, we reached the Deep Woods and this Skull Cave. Now with the Chiefs of the Jungle and the Lords of the Misty Mountains in attendance, not forgetting his Majesty the Ottoman Sultan Abu Mahoud who came with a rich and mighty retinue, I married the beauteous Heloise of Hanta. It was a splendid wedding that left the entire jungle drunk for a week.

"Heloise, now the loyal wife of my bosom, has made one request—that we return to the ruined castle of Koqania to spend one night together in that cell where I had been incarcerated. There is also a casket of her finest jewels cached near this cell, which she believes might have survived the destruction of the castle. I must add she has no regrets on that score. She inherited it all from her father, a notorious buccaneer, and is happy to be rid of it.

"So we shall return for a last visit to Koqania, for a night of love, a delayed honeymoon, in that cell where I languished by order of the notorious witch of Hanta."

The account, written in the fine hand on both sides of the vellum, ended there. Why had it been torn out of the chronicle? No Phantom would do it. Only one person could have. Heloise herself, wishing to leave this account of her marriage in that cell where she had pleaded and wept and protested her love, and now would celebrate it. A sentimental woman, he decided. No, not like Greta.

At a much later time, when telling Diana Palmer the entire story of the witches of Hanta, he said, "Diana, I knew that Heloise, that first witch of Hanta, was not really a witch all along."

"And how, Oh mysterious stranger, did you know that?" asked Diana.

"Because in the chronicle, the part about her weeping at the bars of his cell. It is well known that real witches have no tears. They cannot cry."

"I must remember that," said Diana, with a bewitching smile.

CHAPTER 24

When Old Mozz finished telling his abridged version of the Hanta witch tales, both old and new, to Rex and Tomm, the boys thought about it for a time. The two ten-year-olds, white and black, were seated on the ground near the Skull Throne. Old Mozz sat on a stump, leaning on his ancient polished cane.

"Did you like the stories?" he asked, knowing the answer would be yes. It always was.

"Yes, but—" said Rex.

"Yes, but what?" said Old Mozz in surprise.

"The Hanta witches weren't real witches. They were pretend witches," said Rex, and Tomm nodded in agreement.

"So the Phantom would have us believe," said Old Mozz with a wink.

"I mean, I hoped they'd be real witches," Rex said, and Tomm nodded. "They were just pretend, weren't they?"

"So the Phantom would have you believe," said the old man, winking again, but neither agreeing or disagreeing. "He asked that I tell you the tale of the Gooley-Gooley witch."

"Is that another pretend witch?"

"That is a real witch," said Old Mozz.

"How real?" said Tomm suspiciously.

"A real witch a thousand years old."

"Really? A thousand years old?" said Rex excitedly.

The old man nodded solemnly.

"And did this happen to the sixth Phantom or the eighth Phantom, or one of those Phantoms way back there?" continued Rex.

"No, this is a tale of the Phantom you know as Uncle Walker, and as time flies, it was not long ago."

Old Mozz looked at the two young faces, both eager and expectant. They were ready. He took a sip of spring water from the wooden bucket in the shade, then began in his singsong voice.

"The Gooley-Gooley witch lived in an old castle atop a peak in the Misty Mountains, which is eastward of here, where the sun rises," began Old Mozz.

"Do all witches live in castles on top of peaks?" asked Rex.

"Those do who can afford it," replied Old Mozz.

"Don't interrupt," said Tomm.

"She was very old, this witch, a thousand years old, and she lived with her familiar spirits, her demons and her monsters, and none in the jungle dared to voyage near this peak, for it was an evil place," continued Old Mozz. "And all the sickness and bad luck of the people was known to be caused by the old witch, but none dared go near her, for she was an evil woman.

"Now as she neared her thousandth birthday, she felt lonely, for she was bored with her familiar spirits, her demons and her monsters. And she decided she would have a mate."

"A mate?" said Tomm excitedly.

"A husband," said Rex. "Shh, go on."

"So the old witch sat before her long magic mirror, and she said to this mirror which could only show things as they really are, 'Mirror, show to me the three most beautiful men in the world.' And one after another, the mirror showed her these three men. The first was a strong man who could lift great weights and wrestle opponents to the earth. A mighty man was he, with arms like big tree boughs, and legs like the trunk of an oak. 'He will not do,' said she. The second was an actor, one who performed before the people. He had long flowing hair, smooth skin and the face and body of a young god. His was a beauty adored by countless women. 'He will not do,' said she. And the third was one with raven locks whose likeness was sought and copied by workers in stone, by painters, by men who made pictures in boxes. He was called a model, and was said by all to be the most prized. 'He will not do,' she said.

" 'Beauty is not enough,' she told her mirror, her familiar spirits, her demons and her monsters; for all were crowded in the room to see what she would see. 'For I would tire of that in a century or less. Mirror that shows things as they are, show me among all men of great achievement, those three who are best.' And the mirror showed her three such men, one after the other.

"The first man was one who had discovered hidden secrets of the earth and the sky. He had flowing white hair and the wisdom of the ages in his eyes. He was called a scientist. 'He will not do,' she said. Next, the mirror brought the image of a small man wearing only a white robe and sandals, a shy and gentle man. Behind him in the mirror, one could see multitudes, for this religious leader had founded a new religion and millions hailed him as their savior. 'He will not do,' she said. The third man was tall and broad-shouldered. He had a stem face, and wore a uniform that glittered with many medals. This was a general who had won a war and subjugated an entire people, a man of power and decision. 'He will not do,' she said. 'What could I talk about to such men?' she asked her familiar spirits, her demons, and her monsters. 'I care nothing for science, religion, or war. I would tire of such in far less than a century.'

"Now the witch asked her mirror to show other men—artists, inventors, athletes, millionaires, billionaires, barons, counts, princes, kings. With each, she found something that would not do for her. As she explained to the impatient creatures about her: 'After a thousand years, one becomes hard to please.' Then she said, 'I have exhausted the various categories and still have not found the perfect man I seek. What shall I ask for now?' And said her familiar spirit, in the shape of a cat, 'Ask for the perfect man.' The old witch clapped her hands for joy.

" 'Mirror that shows things as they really are, show to me the man most perfect of all men,' she said. And the mirror showed her this man.

"And who do you think it was?" asked Old Mozz.

"Uncle Walker," said Rex excitedly.

"Precisely, the Phantom," said Old Mozz.

"And the witch said, 'He appears to be a fine specimen indeed, but who is he?' And her familiar spirits, demons, and monsters told her, for between them, they knew all things. 'Then bring him before me so that I may see him with my own eyes and decide if this will indeed be my mate,' said the Gooley-Gooley witch.

"So her familiar spirit journeyed to the Deep Woods, not in the shape of a cat, but as a courtier in silks and satins. He was brought before this very Skull Throne and, with a deep bow, invited the Phantom to visit his mistress. Politely, but firmly, the Phantom refused. The courtier was shocked. No one refused an invitation from his mistress, he told him. 'Then this will be the first time,' said the Phantom.

"That sounds like him," said Rex.

"The courtier returned to his mistress, becoming a cat again as soon as he was out of sight. The witch was furious. She hurled curses that shook the walls and withered flowers for a half mile around. But this made her even more eager to behold this man. So she sent a second invitation. This invitation arrived with the same courtier and three camels loaded with gifts. These gifts were chests of diamonds, rubies and emeralds, pieces of gold, riches beyond belief."

"Uncle Walker didn't need that. He's got all he wants in the cave."

"Shh," said Tomm. "Go on please, Uncle Mozz."

"Once again, the Phantom refused the invitation, and when the caravan had left the Deep Woods and was out of sight, the treasure turned to dung and the camels to great creepy hairy things.

"Now the witch's fury was even greater than before. She hurled curses that withered leaves from the trees and birds from their nests for a mile around. 'Go back again,' she shouted.

"Now came the third and last invitation. A caravan of milk-white horses drawing carriages, and in every carriage were the most beautiful women one could imagine. All in gold and lace and sparkling jewels. Their teeth were white and their eyes sparkled with unfulfilled love.

" 'My mistress begs you accept these handmaidens as a token of her esteem and asks that you visit her castle!' said the courtier."

"Now what would Uncle Walker do with all those women?" said Rex scornfully. "That was a silly gift."

"Shh," said Tomm. "Go on, please."

"Once again," continued Old Mozz, "the Phantom refused and the milk-white horses and carriages departed. Once out of sight, the beauteous maidens and horses turned into demons and monsters, for that is what they really were, and the carriages turned into dung. And this evil host flew back to the castle, where their mistress awaited, and her fury was terrible to behold. Now she hurled curses that destroyed birds in the air and small animals on the ground for a mile around.

" 'Thrice he has refused me. Now shall I make no more offers. But let this be known. Unless he comes to me of his own free will, then shall the first born of the chief of each village sicken and die.' And from her high balcony overlooking the Misty Valley far below, she hurled this curse. And that curse went like a bolt of lightning into all the villages of the jungle.

"The Phantom was told of the curse, but he laughed and said the old witch could not do that. But as time passed, the eldest son of the chief in each village did sicken and lose his strength. And the chiefs came to that Phantom and told him of this and said, 'O Ghost Who Walks, if you do not visit the Gooley-Gooley witch, our eldest sons will surely die.' And he saw this was true.

"Now the Phantom was angry, and he mounted upon his great white stallion Hero and raced through the jungle to the Misty Mountains. And all the jungle knew his mission, and prayed for his success.

"The witch, on her high balcony over the Misty Valley, saw him approaching with the speed of the wind, and she was prepared. He rode up the stairs, then burst into the great hall, ready to do battle with the evil witch as best he could.

"He was greeted by a woman wondrously beautiful. Her hair was black, her eyes dark, her skin pale, and she gleamed with magnificent jewels that hung from her long graceful throat, and encircled her waist, arms, and ankles. Though he did not know it, this was a woman of ancient times named Nefertiti of Egypt, in her lifetime queen of that place and acclaimed the most beautiful woman in the world. Her voice was soft and warm as she spoke, for she was happy with what she saw.

" 'Phantom, I have waited so long for you,' said she.

"The Phantom was surprised. This was not the woman he expected. 'I am told that through your curse the eldest sons of the chiefs sicken and die. Can this be true?'

" 'It was my wish to bring you here,' said she.

" 'Why did you wish to bring me here?' asked he.

" 'Can you not guess?' she said, extending her arms to him. (Old Mozz acted out all these movements, extended his arms to the enthralled boys.) 'I am lonely here. I yearn for a worthy mate. My mirror found you.' The long mirror was now covered with a golden cloth. The Phantom looked in astonishment at it, then at her, for nothing she might have said could have surprised him more.

" 'I thank you,' he said, for he was always a courteous man. 'But I have a girl whom I love.' "

"Diana," whispered Rex.

"Shh," said Tomm.

" 'I will make you forget all other women,' said this beauty of the Nile.

" 'Free those eldest sons from your curse so they may live,' he said. And she agreed, for she said, 'I put that curse upon them so you would come here of your own free will, and so you have.' And she stepped upon her high balcony over the Misty Valley and waved her beautiful arms and she uttered incantations. And in each village, the eldest sons were suddenly well and strong, and even in this castle high on the peak, they could hear the sounds of happiness below.

" 'Thank you. Now I will go,' said the Phantom, and turned to the door.

" 'Wait!' said she. 'Did I not please you? Is this more to your taste?' And he turned and was amazed to see that she was no longer Nefertiti of the Nile, but all pink and white and fluffy, a beauty in silks and satins from the court of the French king.

" 'I cannot stay, I must go,' said the Phantom, for this transformation was confusing to him. But as he neared the door, a third voice spoke to him, and a tender hand touched his shoulder. And he turned to see the most beautiful woman of all. Her hair was long and blonde, her eyes the deepest blue, her skin fairer than any white cloud, her body a poet's dream. For this was Helen of Troy of whom the poets sang, for whom men fought a war, for whom a nation fell. It is said that of all woman before and after her, none was as beautiful as this Helen of Troy.

"And now her soft hands touched his face, and her voice was sweet and gentle, and it must be said that no man, not even the Phantom, could resist this Helen. For a moment, a long moment, he was captured by her, ready to give up the world and all he knew for this most perfect of women. But as he embraced her and felt her rub softly against him, some little inner voice saved him, perhaps a friendly spirit, perhaps an ancestor. He held her by her perfect arms and took her to the long, covered mirror.

" 'Let me see you in your mirror that shows things as they really are,' he said. 'No!' she pleaded, tears falling from her beautiful eyes, her perfect red lips whispering promises of eternal love. But he closed his eyes to shut out this tempting vision, this most beautiful and desirable woman who ever lived on this earth, and with one great sweep of his hand, he tore off the golden cloth to reveal the mirror.

"And there, in that mirror that showed things as they really are, he saw the Gooley-Gooley witch as she really was. A thousand years old, her living skeleton showing through her withered flesh. Now the creature at his side, no longer beauteous Helen, shrieked curses and maledictions. The walls and ceiling shook, lightning flashed, thunder roared, and the familiar spirits, demons, and monsters poured into the great hall.

" 'Kill him, kill him,' she shrieked, and they went at him all together, the flying demons, and crawling things and monstrous shapes. And they bit and clawed and battered and slashed. But using all his mighty strength, he battled them. He battled his way through that howling mob of familiar spirits, demons, and monsters and reached the doors of the great hall. Down the stairs he ran, with the creatures after him. He leaped upon Hero, his great white stallion, and raced down the mountainside. But the creatures stopped at the bottom stair, for that was as far as they could go.

"Now as the thunder roared, the lightning flashed, and the very earth shook, he raced down that steep slope. And above on the high balcony, the ancient witch stood, her arms stretched out to him crying, 'Phantom, Phantom, come back to me.' He did not heed, but raced on. Then as he neared the safety of the jungle, he looked back once more to see her on that balcony high above the Misty Valley, with her creatures swarming about her as she cried. And there was a tremendous explosion and flash of light and the entire castle disappeared into nothing as though it had never been there. It was gone, and all that inhabited that evil place were gone with it.

"But it is said," concluded Old Mozz, "that each year on the night of All hallows eve, that night when the demons soar in the upper air, the castle appears atop the peak, and there upon the balcony one can see for a brief moment, the Gooley-Gooley witch, surrounded by her familiar spirits, her demons, and her monsters, as she stretches out her ancient withered arms and cries in piteous tones, 'Phantom, Phantom, come back to me.' "

That was the end of it. "Did that really happen?" said Rex, dazed by this story.

"As I told you."

"But what else?" said Tomm.

Old Mozz remained silent like a statue. The story was finished. There was nothing else to be said. At that moment, the Phantom himself rode slowly toward the Skull Cave on Hero. He dismounted, waved to them, and walked toward the Skull Throne. The two boys stared at him, for once in their young lives, speechless.

WITH THE PHANTOM, EVERYTHING IS POSSIBLE— EXCEPT BOREDOM

by
Francis Lacassin, Lecturer
The Sorbonne, Paris, France

When Lee Falk introduced into comic-strip format the imaginary and the fantastic with the figure of *Mandrake, The Magician*, it was apparent that he was contributing to what I describe to my students at the Sorbonne as "The Ninth Art." It was even more evident when he invented The Phantom, a figure who set the fashion for the masked and costumed Man of Justice,

On November 15, 1971, the oldest university in Europe, the Sorbonne, opened its doors to the comics. I was privileged to give, with the section of Graphic Arts, a weekly two-hour course in the History of the Aesthetics and Language of Comic Strips. Prior sessions had been devoted to the *Phantom*. The female students were drawn to the attractiveness and elegance of his figure; the men liked his masculinity and humor. To me, Lee Falk's stories— representing as they do the present-day *Thousand and One Nights*, fairy tales, *The Tales of the Knights of the Round Table*, etc.—adapt the epic poetry for the dreams and needs of an advanced and industrial civilization. For me the Phantom reincarnates Achilles, the valorous warrior of the Trojan War, and like a knight he wanders about the world in search of a crime to castigate or a wrong to right.

Lee Falk's art of storytelling is defined as much by the succinctness of the action, as by that of the dialogue. The text has not only a dry, terse quality, but also delicious humor. The humor shows itself in the action by the choice of daring ellipses: nothing remains but the strong points of the action. This allows the story to progress more rapidly and reduces the gestures of the hero to those which underlie his fantastic physical prowess. Falk gives the drama in a nutshell. A remarkable example is the resume done in four frames (in the comic strip) and placed at the beginning of each episode to recall the Phantom's origins. In four pictures, everything about the man is said, his romantic legend, his noble mission. Moreover, the new reader enters the fabulous world of Lee Falk, where nothing is real but everything is possible—except boredom.

Dressed in a soft hat and an overcoat with the collar upturned, the Phantom and his wolf, Devil, wander about the world, the cities of Europe, or, dressed in his eighteenth-century executioner's costume, he passes his time in the jungle. Wherever he is, he acts like a sorcerer of the fantastic. Under his touch, the real seems to crack and dreams Well through.

A masked ball in the Latin Quarter appears. In the Phantom's eyes it is the rendezvous of a redoubtable secret society of women. The jungle vegetation becomes the jewel box in which are hidden lost cities, sleeping gods, vampire queens, tournaments worthy of the Olympic Games. The geography, the flowers, the animals in their turn undergo a magical change brought on by the hero. A savage continent borders the edge of the *Deep Woods*. It is protected by a praetorian guard, the pygmies. The Skull Cave contains the treasures of war and the archives of his ancestors. All this occurs on a mythical continent which is not exactly Africa nor exactly Asia, because the tigers and lions are friends.

The genius of Lee Falk is to have known how to create a new *Odyssey*, with all of its fantastic color, but what is even more surprising is that it would be believable in the familiar settings of the modern world. The Phantom acts with the audacity of Ulysses and also with the nobility of a knight-errant. In contrast to Ulysses, and similarly to Sir Lancelot, he moves about in the world of his own free will among his peers. Lee Falk has not only managed to combine epic poetry with fairy tales and the stories of chivalry, he has made of the Phantom, in a jungle spared by colonialism, an agent of political equilibrium and friendship between races. In giving his hero an eternal mission, Lee Falk has made him so real, so near, so believable that he has made of him a man of all times. He will outlive him as Ulysses has outlived Homer. But in contrast to Ulysses, his adventures will continue after his creator is gone, because his creator has made of him an indispensable figure endowed with a life of his own. This is a privilege of which the heroes of written word cannot partake; no one has been able to imitate Homer.

However, the comic strip is the victim of a fragile medium, the newspaper. Because of this, some adventures of *The Phantom* have been lost and live only in the memory of their readers. This memory is difficult to communicate to others. Lee Falk has, therefore, given a new dimension to *The Phantom* by making of him the hero of a series of novels, introducing his origins and his first adventures to those who did not know him before.

This is not his least important accomplishment, but the most significant in my opinion is this: —in presenting to us The Phantom, as a friend Lee Falk has taught us to dream, which is something no school in the world can teach.

Francis Lacassin
June, 1972 Paris

COMING SOON FROM HERMES PRESS

Volume 13: The Island of Dogs!